Ray Anthony was born in Kingston Jamaica in 1958 and lived with his grandparents until 1968, when he came to Britain to join his parents. Educated in south London, when he had the choice, he studied only maths and science - he found the arts crushingly boring. His first employment was in retail management, then he joined the Royal Air Force. After leaving the Royal Air Force he changed career to media sales management. It was during this time that he discovered he had a hidden creative bent. *'Less of my time was being spent on selling or managing, and more on shuffling pieces of paper. Writing strategic reports did my brain in, so I started [j]azzing them up'. The bosses were not amused. If I wanted to keep my job* and *my sanity, I had to find some release.'* In 1987 he started writing his first novel. He is now a media sales consultant and finds that training salespeople gives him ample scope to exercise his theatrical predisposition.

Also by Ray Anthony

Science Fiction
Interdictor - *Book One of* The Unknowable Enemy *Trilogy*
Captain - *Book Three of* The Unknowable Enemy *Trilogy*
Pilot
Empress

Contemporary Fiction
All Woman
Interface

Non Fiction Humour
Thinking Man's Guide To Pregnancy, Childbirth & Fatherhood

ARMOUR

The Unknowable Enemy

BOOK TWO

Ray Anthony

ACE - London

Copyright © Ray Anthony 2016

All rights reserved

ISBN 978 1 8382975 2 7

ACE

PO Box 10289

London SW17 9ZF

www.acebooksonline.com

Chapter 1

"Basche, Bataa. Private. Air Calvary. Echo, tango, nine, three, seven, seven, two, six. Diagnostics: main power level, twelve percent - charging; auxiliary power level, twenty-six percent - charging; all bio systems stable; communications, all channels functioning. Combat ready in T minus eighteen minutes." As soon as he had it racked the suit started chatting to him. Why? As he'd just stepped out of it, it wasn't telling him anything he didn't already know. Mind you, that twelve percent power level underlined just what a busy boy he'd been.

He detached the suit's key, it stopped glowing and he pocketed it as he done innumerable time before. Except this time along the aisle, strolling towards him came Spam, or to use her official title, Sergeant Brotzmann, the section leader. More troublingly she wore an expression that said she was either trying very hard not to laugh or not to cry. Either scenario would be a conveyer of extremely bad tidings because Spam's was a face that didn't, as a rule, do laughter or tears. A slight tilt of her head and her unfocussed eyes hinted that she was still in comms via her earpiece. Halting in front of him she looked down into his eyes. Despite being over two metres tall himself he found himself yet again considering that in all of human history there couldn't have been that many women who were over two and half metres tall.

"Smiler, make safe and proceed to Hopper Bay 7."

Oh dear! This was going to be beyond bad tidings. He didn't know how Spam got that name, she was a Sergeant after all, but in calling him Smiler she was conveying that she was simply the messenger and didn't know any more than she was telling him. He got the name 'Smiler' in boot camp after explaining that whatever region on Earth his great grandmother was from, her name meant 'Of the Beaming Smile' in the local language… on reflection if he hadn't reacted so heatedly to the slight against his beloved, and recently deceased, Emee that nickname probably wouldn't have stuck.

They both set off for the weapons rack two tiers below. Whatever awaited him at Hopper Bay 7 he needed to have his personal weapon with him but… Drop divisions always jumped suited & booted and the Jump Suites used by the infantry were invariably near the Hopper Bays and armouries. Although it was Standard Operating Procedures to check and then double check weapons unloaded before entering Suites, Bays, Hoppers, or armouries these areas, and connecting corridors between them, still had hardened protection against a negligent discharge. Mind you the punishment for any such negligent discharge was pretty damn severe.

Away from these reinforced spaces anyone carrying a weapon had to make it safe so that even the most causal glimpse would explicitly show the weapon to be not only unloaded but disassembled and incapable of being fired. Otherwise the assumption would be made that you'd 'gone rouge' and you'd discover that there are situations where no questions were asked and that the military have a very specific interpretation of the word 'expedite'… This just didn't make sense; he was being sent to an unspecified destination with his rifle but without his combat suit.

As they stepped off the open elevator, he suspected that it was 'laugh'. This was confirmed when they arrived at their weapons rack because he spotted a definite glint in her eye. It wasn't an accident that they always racked weapons first;

without the suit's strength augmentation hefting the twenty-eight-kilogram laser was, to say the least, challenging.

Stepping up to him she bawled into his face, "Make safe!"

Yep, Spam was trying her darndest to avert wetting herself with laughter. The first movement of the drill was, with the barrel point vertically up, to present the vacant energy pack chamber to her. And his muscles started to protest. Then, with the barrel still vertical he placed the butt on his thigh, detached the superconducting coil and held it up for her inspection. Next, he positioned the laser over his shoulder with the barrel pointing backwards thus allowing her to easily inspect the hologrammatic sight displaying only standby energy stored.

Taking a smart backward pace, she confirmed, "The weapon is safe!"

Loosening the strap, he slung the laser over his back, barrel pointing down, and then took the superconducting coil in both hands as if carrying a baton - in plain sight for all to see.

"Do you know the route to Hopper Bay 7?" she inquired mildly.

He supposed that in some quarters this would pass for gallows humour as he didn't even know which ship he was on. Then again this could, under certain circumstances, pass for camaraderie seeing as they were the only unscathed survivors of their twelve-man section; five of them had actually made it off planet but it would be a while before any of the other three would be capable of walking. Rather than taking the bait he just looked up at her. She simply stood there on the gantry staring back at him.

This impasse was totally in keeping with the month he'd been having. It had started with a warning order that their entire fleet was being subsumed into the second fleet. Yes, he was less than bottom feeding pond life but even he'd heard of Admiral Akobundu-Tan and her second fleet. What he'd pick up was, on a regularly basis, they had been handed a seriously good hiding at the hand of the Bulges. Yet she always went back for more. Now here she was being given command of a task force. Wasn't this a prima facia case of rewarding failure?

His opinion wasn't sought or heeded because he and his Air Calvary brigaded were transferred to the recently commissioned assault transport *Carmarthen* that, as luck would have it, was earmarked to be part of the first assault wave. Of course, once this kind of luck found you it tended to stick around. For instance, when they got into the intense round-the-clock battle sims and briefings for the Omega Zero Three op it became pretty clear that the Air Calvary divisions were going to be first boots on the ground. And, wouldn't you just know it, his brigade was going to be amongst the first of the first.

Unlike the marines who tended to 'jump' the Air Calvary, being considerably more heavily armed, 'landed'. It was dawn planetside when his Hopper, in marked contrast to its frenzied atmospheric manoeuvrings, softly touched down. His platoon disembarked at the double and straight into a firefight. Although they had been briefed on the Bulge-mound-column connection it wasn't until you actually saw it kicking off that you 'comprehended' - totally weird or what? Whereas a marine would think eight mortars a surfeit an Air Calvary trooper wouldn't get out of bed with less than a dozen. So, there you are up to your eyes in Bulges and, for the first time, achieving a modicum of success… Hang on a sec, how do you measure success in all that murderous insanity? Does the word in fact have any meaning in a situation like that planetside on Omega Zero Three?

His personal measure of success was being resupplied not once but twice. Obviously they practised resupply drills: you had to be slick with getting ammo off, and casualties on to, Hoppers - they were vulnerable when on the ground and you also needed to keep the enemy fully occupied. But, in his not inconsiderable experience, resupplying had been only a theoretical scenario and the drills were just more military make-work. Why? Because every time his, and as far as he knew any, Air Calvary division went up against the Bulges they got mauled and were executing a hasty withdrawal long before using up even a tiny fraction of their ammo.

He was twenty-four-years-old and had been a soldier all his adult life (not that conscripts had any choice in the matter) therefore he couldn't help feeling that handing the Bulges some payback was long overdue. Just as the payback started to garner some serious compound interest the call came for a full-scale lift. Why? To his knowledge in the twenty-seven years since they'd shown up there had been no engagement with the Bulges that the Saps had come close to holding their own let alone start to win. Now they were being lifted. Had Akobundu-Tan completely lost her marbles? By the time they had made it to orbit he'd gathered over the general comms chatter, the Bulges had blown up the planet. Yes, really, the whole planet. This, he thought, was somewhat churlish of the aliens.

One Hopper Bay was pretty much the same as any other, but he made an educated guess that they weren't on a transporter because their Bays tended to be considerably larger than the norm. They debussed then spent the next forty-five minutes or so suited and booted, strapped down, in a Jump Suite before the ship actually jumped. The rumour-mill had said, 'combat sweeps' but he wasn't that engaged, he was still grappling with the concept of totalling a planet.

"No, I don't," he relented.

A hologram schematic of the interior of a ship appeared between them. "Here's Armoury 4 and here's Hopper Bay 7."

Both Armoury and Hopper Bay were emphasised as she spoke.

The schematic showed that they were on was the corvette *Incantagione* and Armoury and Bay were about 300 metres apart. The ship would no doubt be packed to the rafters with the unwashed and he really didn't fancy lugging a laser through all that…

"You're being transferred."

Transferred?! You survived, or you got killed, or you got maimed; in the latter two instances some wide-eyed fresh-faced teenager comes a-rolling off the production line to take your place. What's left of you or any of your parts that can be identified is returned to your love-ones. That was it. They were the only options. Soldiers never got transferred.

"Transferred to where?"

"Dunno, not even the Colonel knows." There was ambivalence written all over Spam's face. On the one hand only a Stinger-like, you are about to be sacrificed, state of affairs could possibly lead to being transferred - this was the sort of highly entertaining event that one could dine out on for months. On the other hand, he had been in Spam's section for over a year and in the Air Calvary that was considered a lifetime - so this was goodbye.

"Head down, arse flat, hug the ground." The hologram disappeared and he wasn't that surprised when she stepped up and tearfully pulled him into an embrace. After you've seen hundreds of your comrades literally blasted out of existence or mutilated beyond recognition you tended not to form close friendships. Still, it wasn't that surprising that he found himself tearfully returning the hug.

***

How many hundreds of times had he been in or out of a Hopper Bay? Yet here he was standing at the entrance to Hopper Bay 7 for over a minute, greatly frustrated, trying to identify the palm reader. There were what appeared to be several sensors around the entrance but nothing that even vaguely resembled a palm reader. Of course he could ask a passing matlow but he'd rather take a buggering-'til-he-bled than profess ignorance to one of them. How the hell do you actually get the doors to open?

"Retina scan," some disembodied automatic eventually decided to inform him.

It also had the good sense to make the scanning interface glow. Just as well because he would have spent several more minutes puzzling over that interface too. He was finding it hard to believe that beyond being able to identify his DNA from body parts his biometrics would be stored anywhere - surely he was simply not important enough for his retina patterns to have been recorded. He stepped up to the interface. What was the protocol? Did it matter which eye? Gingerly he lent forward and offered his right eye.

The iris door opened with a slight hiss. Hesitantly he stepped into the dimly lit Bay and noted that there were scores of Hoppers parked like giant sleeping beasts. Even on corvette sized ship the Bay was still a respectable two hundred and fifty by seventy-five by fifty metre cuboid. He was immediately subjected to a feeling of rising panic. The door of the nearest Hopper swung open invitingly while he stood rooted to the spot swaying, the feeling of panic had increased alarmingly, and it was now accompanied by a slight dizziness and nausea. Then with implacable timing the Bay door closed behind him with a sinister whisper.

Just before he started retching something deep within his intellect supplied the answer: rampant agoraphobia. If he'd been on a planet this wouldn't be happening but, on a spaceship, the one thing there was never enough of was 'space'. Troop carriers commenced missions with three battalions per zone on rolling eight hour stints: eight hours combat prepping, eight hours R & R, eight hours hot bunking - trying to sleep (and you always took the opportunity to sleep when it presented itself) with some other person's body odour ripe your nostrils.

A ridiculous amount of logistical effort was expended in ensuring that one of the hot bunking triplets was of the opposite sex. Apparently, this was an aid to mental wellbeing: all male pheromones *bad*, all female pheromones *bad*. He was no scientist but as far as he was concerned there was no upside to sleeping in covers reeking of a female. Whoever had come up with that crap ought to be taken somewhere and beaten senseless with a blunt instrument.

Having a monstrous hard-on when you're lying in a bunk that you didn't have exclusively rights to meant you couldn't be as free with it as you'd like - not a good place to be. And that's was without getting into the slight, but noteworthy, issue of there never being any privacy anyway. Of course, a woman could be much more discreet about these matters. This was all fine and dandy until it was you who next had to get into the same enclosed zero-G cocoon, euphemistically referred to as a bunk, after she'd released whatever tensions she needed to release... No, they should be flayed alive!

That was on the way out. On the way back, if you were one of the lucky few to make it back, it was worse - much worse. Although there could be millions of infantry dead there was always a higher percentage of ships lost. It didn't matter what they called it, it was always full-scale, run as fast as you can, chaotic, retreat. Overfill! Every nook, cranny, and spare square metre on the *space*ship bursting at the seams with the walking wounded. Yet no matter how overcrowded the ship, the conditions escalated to the inhumane just before it jumped. He'd never thought it possible to sleep standing upright but in actual fact it was easy to do when packed in so tightly into a Jump Suite that standing bolt upright was the only option. Which just goes to show that all things are relative: there are situations where you'd give your right hand to be enclosed in a cocoon redolent of stale vaginal odours.

Steadying himself he headed for the Hopper and entered. Still far too much vacant space; Hoppers usually carried a fully armed combat-ready platoon. As he stood there wondering what to do next, he spotted his bergan and kitbag already on board, racked and stored. The last time he'd seen this gear, containing pretty much the sum total of his life's possessions, it was on board a transport called *Carmarthen* that probably no longer existed.

With a peripatetic lifestyle resulting from the gung-ho attitude of 'regiments never die' the infantryman quickly learned to travel light: three quarters of a unit decimated? No problem, simply shunt in more bodies with their kit and caboodle. It could have been worst, had he been a marine he would have a lot more crap to lug around - they had ceremonial duties onboard ships and appeared to need a different uniform for each occasion. Still, here before his very eyes was his kit. The probability of such an occurrence in a combat fleet that had only just fought a major battle was mind-bending.... *Hmm, interesting and very disquieting.*

What he would usually do on entering a Hopper was sit and strap in with the rest of his company. Without his suit's strength augmentation, the rifle was far too heavy for him to hold as he usually would, so he strapped it to the seat on his right. As he sat and started to strap himself in, the door closed silently. No! A Hopper journey with only one passenger? He surfed around in his memories for a while: no recollection of even ever hearing about anything remotely like that. This was breaking the bounds of common sense and energy efficiency.

How do you launch a Hopper? Not a question he'd ever had reason to ask. Presumably the officers gave the Hopper's automatics some kind of verbal instruction. Most probably this would be done on a command frequency. That would explain why he didn't even know where to begin… Without fuss the Hopper lifted and started taxiing towards the space doors. It would be pointless to try and guess how many times he'd been inside a Hopper as it exited a carrier embarking on either a mission or a slightly less fraught combat exercise. Yet he couldn't think of a single occasion where he'd paid the slightest attention to the egress process. Normally he would be totally preoccupied with three things: suppressing fear to the point where it wasn't debilitating, fretting about not letting his comrades down and remembering the multitude of things he needed to remember about the particular mission or exercise.

Leisurely. Not a world he'd normally associate with a Hopper transit but as it exited into the star-splattered blackness all was very calm and serene. Wherever here was, was close enough to a nearby star that he actually got a chance, and had the time, to give the corvette *Incantagione* the once over. Though he'd never considered himself an expert on spaceship aesthetics the adjective 'handsome' came to mind: she was elegantly proportioned with sleek flowing lines. It was also obvious that she was quite tiny by the usual standards. The big boys tended to be hideous monstrosities - all protruding railguns and laser batteries interspaced with missile launching fissures. Despite the elegance, *Incantagione* clearly hadn't ducked out of anything because there were potted scorch marks all along the side visible to him.

So taken was he with the examination of the pretty little ship that he was surprised at suddenly finding his Hopper slipping into another slightly bigger Bay - not a carrier but bigger than a corvette he guessed. Again, this Bay was dimly lit, crammed with Hoppers and, as far as he could tell, devoid of personnel. As the craft taxied, he modified his assessment of being the Bay's sole occupant. Over to the left and about fifty metres ahead was another taxiing Hopper that seemed to have entered from a different space door only seconds before. His Hopper then manoeuvred to tuck in behind as the other craft led the way... Hmm seems to be a joint destination. Along one wall in big bold letters was stencilled 'Bay 12B.' Time for a reassessment; it must be a pretty big ship to have at least 12 hopper bays. Not as big as a carrier but still big - a cruiser or heavy cruiser then, he'd never been on a cruiser. Yet Bay 12B still seemed to be on the smallish side; smaller than *Incantagione's.*

The other Hopper settled down in the parking spot closest to a Bay door and it was obvious that his vehicle was heading for the space right next to it. As the door of the other Hopper opened a sailor's holdall was tossed out followed in short order by a kitbag. He was just starting to conjecture about untypically untidy matlows when a guy stepped out with a rifle slung across his back and a bergan in his hand - not matlows, marines. The door of the other Hopper closed just as his touched down. He remained in his seat for a few seconds, speechless: two Hoppers with single passengers. The last hours or so was redefining what he thought of as credible or realistic.

With a marine around *form* was going to be important; he pulled himself together, gathered his bits and made sure that his unflustered exit was with rifle and bergan on his back and kitbag and superconducting coil in his hands. He strolled up to the marine: same rank - Private, same build, about four centimetres shorter, very dark skinned but with serious epicanthic folds making his eyes seem like mere slits.

"Bataa." Then he transferred kitbag and superconducting coil to one hand and calmly reached down to take one handle of the holdall with the other - well, how often do you get the opportunity to out-cool a marine.

"Rafiu." The marine rearranged his kit, including the superconducting coil, about himself then reached for the other handle.

On cue, as they hoisted the holdall, the Bay door opened and standing just outside was a master sergeant. Not just any old master sergeant but a Guardsman master sergeant, sunglasses and all. Guardsman: the only other corps to wear one-piece suits along with the Stingers. Where the Stinger black one-piece was feared and grudgingly respected, the Guardsman sky-blue one-piece was universally reviled and ridiculed. You didn't see them that often but even so what kind of screaming arsehole wore sunglasses even in the dark? And why did they always strut about the place with their collars turned up. Although in polite company they were universally referred to a 'Dandies' the more usual epithet was, 'those effin' prigs'.

All that being said, this particular master sergeant was obviously a Vet and like all Vets he exuded an aura of having actually seen things you'd only had nightmares about. "With me, gentlemen," he commanded coolly, spun on his heels, folded his arms behind his back and set of at a casual pace. Having exchanged a questioning glance with Rafiu they followed.

The journey along deserted corridors didn't last that long but they passed the entrances to a Jump Suite, a battle simulator and to somewhere quaintly identified as First Aid. The master sergeant brought them to a halt outside Armoury 12B. Bataa couldn't recall ever seeing an armoury, in space or planet-bound, that wasn't being ostentatiously cossetted by a heavily armed guard. Clearly Rafiu was having a similar response; further furtive questioning glances were exchanged.

The master sergeant placed a hand on a palm reader and the armoury door dilated. "Drop your kit here, rack your weapons."

They did as instructed and entered what turned out to be the smallest armoury, ever. There was only one level and slots to rack, maybe at a pinch, one company. They reassembled their rifles, racked them then both gave the miniscule armoury a cursory inspection. The hand weapons seemed pretty standard but the suspended combat suits looked odd; similar to but, in some undefined way, different to those worn by Stingers.

The master sergeant was striding away before the armoury door had closed behind them. They grabbed their kit and caught up with him just as he stopped outside a nondescript door. Folding his arm, this time arms across his chest, he turned to face them. From behind his sunglasses and with a calm patience he took some time looking them over. Eventually he said, "Gentleman, I am The Quartermaster. Through this door are the stores, beyond that area are two booths. In them you will find your new outfits and a bergan, don one set. *All* of the remainder of your kit and any personal possession must fit into that single bergan. It'll be tough, so take your time." He then stepped smartly aside.

Bataa exchanged a final glance with Rafiu then stepped up to the door that dilated as he approached. To his mind, the term 'booth' suggested something with a door. Having wandered past a miniature 'stores' in front of them were two cubbyholes with their names above them... No, the military wasn't getting all soft, cuddly, and personable. Instinctively he knew that this was something far deeper, in fact, this was looking damn right sinister: after having it beaten out of them at boot camp, why were they being reintroduced to the concept of personal space? Well, at least he now knew Rafiu's surname was Delzoppo.

Stepping into his 'booth' he noted its bleak contents; a single bench with neatly folded garments and a bergan placed on top. As a basic Grunt one got used to not asking questions, but this day of weirdness was beginning to grate. Every item in the stack of clothing was sky blue in colour. He undressed until he was stark bollock naked then sat on the bench next to the outfits, rebellion coursing through his veins - he detested the Dandies and had no wish to become one of them. Bataa let the anger run its course, after all the master sergeant had told them to take their time, he then took up his old bergan. Feeling an unexpected attachment to the carrier he began to empty its neat and compactly packed contents.

Once the bergan was empty, its contents stacked the other side of him, there was only one item that he considered truly personal. It had belonged to his great grandmother and was given to him by his mother the day he left for basic infantry training: an antique leather purse that had the word 'Mongolia' embossed on the flap that was secured with a tie. His mother had taken great pride in explaining, at lengths, the functions of a purse, what leather was and where this particular cut originated. None of her discourse sank in because he had little interest in the animals of Earth and even less in their hides. What he really wanted to know about was this Mongolia - he liked the way the sound rolled off the tongue. Mum either didn't know or didn't care much about Mongolia but from her imperfect explanation he inferred that it was town or city on Earth.

He undid the neatly tied bow, opened the purse, and took out its contents: three data crystals and two wedding rings; the sum total of his personal possessions. One heavily encrypted crystal was the accumulation of personal message from family and friends. In fact, it contained every digital communication from a civilian that he'd decided to keep. And at some indefinable moment he'd realised that he would never know when he was about to draw his last breath, so he decided to keep everything. From time to time, when he had a mind to, he'd browsed the holomessages and immersed himself in nostalgia. The ones from Mengesha, his old sweetheart, he found particularly touching because they were from a time when he was still naive enough to believe that he could maintain a relationship with a woman, light-years distant who, if he was extremely lucky, he might get to see once every two years or so. Back on Trolus, he'd often heard this phenomenon referred to as, 'The optimism of youth.'

Another of the crystals was a chronicle of his combat missions cum digital mementos; be they suit logs, comms recordings, video captures or surface atmospheric readings. He'd been on enough missions on enough planets and moons and been in enough firefights (all-be-it, one-sided firefights, and near-death experiences) to have nearly reached the crystal's voluminous capacity. During an occasional sober reflective mood, he'd chastised himself for instigating such a thoroughly morbid, self-defeating, and obsessive practice, yet it was an entrenched superstitious habit he couldn't kick. In this delusion he wasn't the least bit unusual, almost everyone in the military had a *thing* that was miraculously instrumental in keeping them alive. For instance, he knew, as a substantiated fact, that Spam always went into combat wearing the same pair of knickers and she always wore them back to front.

The third crystal was his mobile office and knowledge repository - work. All the good gen that a Calvary man needed to know but couldn't possibly carry around in his head: want to prep a suit for a sulphur dioxide atmosphere with a mean temperature of 120° C? What is the effective kill range of a standard laser rifle in salt water at seven atmospheres pressure? How do you darn socks made of sheer-proof photocatalytic fibres? Every mission was unique and required detailed preparation, simulations, and recalibrations. As an example, prepping for the preceding op to Omega Zero Three had taken his regiment weeks. And something as simple as dialling in to operating in a one point seven G environment was physically demanding and mentally draining while, at the same time, tedious beyond belief - the third crystal worked overtime.

Along with the purse from his mother he'd been given the two wives' platinum wedding rings, one from each of his dads. When they ceremoniously place them in his open palm, it occurred to him that 'education' had been all about teaching the youth a multitude of things that the youth had absolutely no interest in. For instance, he *knew* that Trolus was a plateaued population planet. It was one of two scores of so-called Earth-like (that is Earth-like as in the Saps could just about tolerate its biosphere) planets that offered, on balance, some economic benefit in its colonisation. The population was allowed to increase - or particularly gullible persons shipped in - until enough of the local produce was being produced then the population was stabilised. He also *knew* that the way to maintain this status quo re: population was to ship out a disproportionate proportion of the fertile females - patrilocation - leading to a polyandric society.

So, he was born on a sparsely populated world whose main contribution to overall human endeavour was the mining and refining of its overabundance of precision metals. In this culture it was quite unremarkable for a woman to have a couple of husband/male partners. It was also perfectly normal to have two fathers, hell, a significant minority of kids had three. Yes, he had been told of places where women did not have multiple partners nor children co-dads. These were the much rarer (even more Earth-like) planets that had the potential of supporting a population in the millions; with a planned geometric population increase, the norm was for men to have multiple wives and children co-moms. He *knew* all this, but, it was all so at odds with his everyday experience that it had gained no purchase on his intellect; he had sought out the term of this implausible practice the first opportunity he got - polygamy.

On reflection it was naively romantic of his dads to present him the wedding bands. On Trolus iridium, platinum, gold and the like were as common as, say, iron but once refined and off planet the cost per gram increased exorbitantly. With polyandry being the norm on the vast majority of planets the rings were simply them edging against him ending up on a polygamous one. Though he loved them dearly he'd never considered either man particularly given to emotional outpouring or being soppy but clearly, in their own way, both were. The chances of him surviving, meeting and then forming a stable long-term relationship with anyone was so vanishing small that marriage, be it a polyandrous match or otherwise, was beyond fantasy. To him the rings were simply a memento of his two loving fathers.

The sound of Rafiu rummaging in his cubical snapped him out of his reverie. Don't swim upstream and roll with the blows because the Man's army was inexorable. Bataa stood, packed his new bergan and started to dress in the loathed Guardsman garments. He really thought that he'd become totally inured to the military shite, but this sky-blue garb was really jarring. By the time he'd finally slipped on the one-piece suit he was praying, sincerely and fervently, that one day he'd meet the individual responsible for this outrage so that he could extract suitable long-lasting retribution.

He'd never seen a Guardsman without his or her collar turned up, so making sure his collar was neatly turned down he grabbed the bergan and stepped out. Moments later Rafiu exited his cubical and his collar was also firmly in the position of 'down'. Hoisting their respective bergans, rebelliously shoulder to shoulder, they stomped out. Arms still folded across his chest the master sergeant was now casually leaning against a wall with his legs crossed. Giving them the once over he smiled thinly then in a friendly, only making a suggestion, tone said, "Gentlemen, collars up."

Master sergeants were, as an entire breed, never friendly. Also, they didn't open their mouths to make 'suggestions'. Both immediately did as they were told. The master sergeant eased himself off the wall and unfolded his arms; in each hand was a pair of sunglasses that he handed to them. "These are your shades, to be worn at all times and all circumstances; the only exception is when you sleep."

They put the sunglasses on. He nodded to their left. "Thirty metres beyond the next right turning is the refectory, fifty metres beyond that are your berths. Briefing tomorrow zero seven hundred, the refectory is also the briefing room. R & R till then." Then he turned and, with a certain unhurried panache, strolled off in the opposite direction.

As soon as he was out of sight, they disobediently yanked off the sunglasses and headed for the 'refectory'. Who, in their right mind, calls a canteen 'the refectory'? Being utter and complete wankers must be a prerequisite to being Dandies…

"You two arseholes, freeze!" A female voice bellowed from behind them.

Stopping and turning simultaneously they saw a group of seven female Dandies, sunglasses and all, striding towards them. They all had that extreme fatigued expression, probably having just left the armoury, after finally being returned to their base ship nearly a day after the Omega Zero Three lift.

Their demeanour screamed 'volatile and irritable'. Five of the Dandies strolled past impolitely brushing them out of the way but neither him or Rafiu reacted to that because the remaining two halted and squared up to them. Both were diminutive, both were 'quite cute', both looked angrier than a seeping open wound. Neither wore insignia or badges of rank.

"You maggots, shades on!" the Dandy facing up to Rafiu bawled at them.

They didn't make the slightest move to comply, but some units never wore rank when 'in the field'… How could such a dissonant utterance have left such a pretty face? And anyway, with masses of blonde hair piled up on her head it was difficult to take her seriously. Long hair in zero G was a hindrance and when wearing the helmet of a combat suit it was pretty risky. Then again most female personnel tended to display some 'I'm a girl' marker. For instance, Spam's marker was bright red lipstick that always clashed ridiculously with the adaptive camouflage.

"Who are you calling a maggot?!" Rafiu spat back. Clearly the marine's pride could only take so much. After all, maggots were fresh-meat, gormless, puss-filled rookies who didn't know one end of a laser rifle from the other.

The leg sweep came out of nowhere and Rafiu was midair, flaying and falling. While Bataa stood considering the most appropriate response the Dandy facing him moved. One moment she was standing a metre from him, the next she was up real close and personal. One hand had a fierce grasp of the front of his suit (and some chest hairs), the sole of one boot was pressing firmly against his stomach, and the sole of the other was planted on his right knee. She made a point of showing that having thus mounted him, while he was still upright, she had a hand free to block anything he'd like to try and, despite the difference in their sizes, she could, if she had a mind to, dislocate his knee without expending any effort.

Blondie was on Rafiu before he hit the deck. He landed immobilised with his neck in a throttling figure-four leglock. She then deftly removed the sunglasses from his top pocket and offhandedly waved them about. "When I say, 'shades on' I mean 'put your fucking shades on', maggot!" She then stuffed them on to his face.

Bataa wasn't even conscious of reacting to the total humiliation of his newfound comrade but the abrupt amplification of the pressure against his right knee hinted that he was. He started to relax but the pressure kept building. His assailant, who was nearly as dark as Rafiu, remained perched on him like some oversized insect until he got the message and, without making any sudden movements, took out his sunglasses and slipped them on. She then sprang off him, landed well outside his immediate strike range and bellowed, "What was your last instruction from The Quartermaster, maggot?!"

Blondie, in a lazy, 'that was all too easy' sort way untangled herself from Rafiu and sprang to her feet. He figured that she and her colleague with the cropped tightly curled black hair were Sergeants. Even so…

"Who, the Hell, are you calling a maggot?" he roared back but despite his best endeavours it was pretty transparent that he was trying to hide acute embarrassment.

The two women exchanged an amused glance before his assailant looked him up and down disdainfully then enquired, "Do you really want me to hurt you?" Pausing as if to give him time to consider this she then added, "Yo mammy ain't here to kiss it better, maggot."

Massaging his neck, Rafiu got back to his feet and Bataa sensed that he was still seething and therefore would back his play…

"Boy, I know what you're thinking," Cropped continued all girly and mischievous. "Make you move by all means, but consider the woe you'll run into having got an arse whipping, to the point of being hospitalised, by a couple of *girls*.

"Who are you calling maggots?" For this attempt he'd tried to sound macho and menacing but it came out high-pitched and wimpish.

"Maggots: wet-behind-the-ears arseholes who because they've been in a scrape or two think they know something worth knowing and can therefore disobey a direct order from The Quartermaster."

Rafiu's head snapped round so fast to focus on her that you heard his neck pop. "A scrape or two?" he asked incredulously, deeply offended and ready to strike.

Blondie crossed her arms and slouched against the wall, much as The Quartermaster had done. "OK, impress us."

"Go fuck yourselves! We don't have to do shit to impress anyone!" Much after-the-fact, Bataa realised he'd shouted rather shrilly.

Blondie eased herself off the wall, strolled right up to him then started circling around as if conducting a detailed parade ground inspection. Her oppo drifted over to Rafiu and proceeded to do exactly the same to him. After a couple of circuits, she halted in front of Rafiu and looked up at him. "Smells like a tyro Marine Commando," she said to no one in particular then added, "Yours?"

"I'm getting a fait whiff of nappy airborne, so probably having wet dreams about being Air Cav when he grows up."

He wasn't consciously aware of throwing the punch. He was only vaguely aware of sailing heels-over-head through the air. He was very definitely aware of slamming into the wall. Another thud, a fraction of a second later, hinted at Rafiu suffering a similar fate. Sliding down the wall he ended up an ungainly crumpled heap on the floor prompting a flashback to his uncoordinated teens. Sensing that, surprisingly, he was uninjured he got back to his feet enraged and spoiling for a fight. Rafiu, clearly having bounced off the opposite wall, was also back on his feet and also good to go. Both women were four or five metres from them which meant…

"You impressed?" Blondie asked of Cropped.

"Must be scraping the absolute bottom of barrel with these two."

Rafiu charged and, reflexively, he took off after him. The corridor wasn't that wide, but like an ultra-slow hologram, both women effortlessly sidestepped their onrush and then rubbed salt into the wound by leaving it at that: signifying that they were so pitiful that neither could be bothered to give them a slap as they whistled past. Skidding to a halt he set himself to charge back, this time gloves off intending to do potentially lethal damage, but Rafiu placed a hand across his chest in restraint.

"Bored," Cropped pronounced then abruptly spun on her heels and strolled off.

Blondie also spun and followed. "They were never *in* the barrel."

Seeing as he had brushed Rafiu's hand out of the way and thus had a head start he was tad surprised when Rafiu reached them before he did. Well, actually, Rafiu didn't exactly 'reach' them. A more accurate description would be 'made it to their approximate vicinity'. To deliver the blow flush on his chin, Cropped had leapt up spinning and for a fleeting moment Rafiu's lower half continued its forward motion whilst his head flew backwards. Bataa was pretty sure he'd never seen anyone move as fast as Cropped had but his awe was rudely interrupted by a thunderous detonation somewhere in his left midriff. This was Blondie's contribution to the discourse and he next found himself sinking to his knees gasping for breath.

Both women appeared undisturbed, disappointedly shaking their heads as they sauntered away. "Maggots!" one of them tutted.

With newfound rage he and Rafiu wobbled back to their feet and like two drunks bumbling along the corridor walls staggered after them. "I'm a first strike assault marine, how many drops have you done you fucking Dandy?!"

Bataa was quite content for Rafiu to take the lead in the speaking role because he was still having difficulties in the breathing department. Bearing in mind the preceding events he was genuinely surprised when both women stopped, turned, and ambled back right up to them - within easy striking range. Placing her head askance Cropped looked Rafiu over then dubiously enquired, "Assault marine you say, really?"

He was scarcely listening; a knife hand strike to the windpip…

"Knife hand strike to my neck?" Blondie teasingly asked. His shock must have been evident because after nonchalantly folding her arms she added, "Noticed you shifting your weight." Leaving a suitable gap, a clear invitation for him to attempt said strike if he so wished, which he declined she then asked, "If he's sayin' 'assault', what you sayin'?"

He sucked in a couple of deep breaths. "Air Cav." It suddenly became rather challenging sustaining unbridled rage at a woman that was this cute.

The women exchanged a glanced then Cropped asked Rafiu, "Last jolly?"

Rafiu took a while in answering and Bataa wouldn't fault him because the sands of this engagement had clearly shifted; but where to? "The Omega Zero Three party."

"You're shitting me!" Cropped mumbled.

Blondie took a pace closer. "And you?"

It took a certain amount of willpower to not react to the blatant invasion of his personal space. "Same."

"Cocksuckers!" Cropped now seemed to be in a severe state of agitation.

"Let me make sure I've got this right: you were on that operation and now you're transferred in?" Blondie's agitation was only a smidgen less. He nodded.

Now it was Cropped's turn to intrude on personal space. "No R & R, no shore leave? Just a, 'Now fuck right off and report to your new unit'?"

Rafiu nodded.

The two women turned to each other aghast and Blondie exclaimed, "Rancid Roger strikes again… You couldn't make this up."

"No, you couldn't," Cropped agreed, swivelled, folded her arms behind her back and strolled off. After several paces she tossed back over her shoulder, "With me, marine." It was a further couple of seconds before Rafiu hesitantly shuffled after her.

Watching them go Blondie waited until they were alone. "It could be argued that one is *entitled* to some down time after a shindig like that planet popping one, wouldn't you say?"

Because he had no idea where this was going, he simply kept his mouth shut and stared back at her and her sunglasses.

"The second door this side of the armoury, it's a storeroom. Be there at twenty-three hundred hours."

He wasn't buying this. "Why?"

"That's unless you prefer boys, of course."

This must be an initiation prank or something along those lines and he'd rather be buggered-'til-he-bled than be out-cooled by a bunch of Dandies. "I meant why twenty-three hundred, what's wrong with right now?"

He hadn't thought that it would be physically possible for her to take another pace closer to him, but she did. Now her breasts were poking him somewhere just above his bellybutton. "I suppose some men like their women with grit under their nails, grime in their hair and absolutely minging like five day worn knickers. Are you one of those, Air Cav?" she purred up at him.

God damn it! Involuntarily he'd stepped back - out-cooled! "Twenty-three hundred hours it is then."

Chapter 2

Entering with other sunglass-wearing, collars turned up, sky blue clad personnel the 'refectory' had been transformed into the smallest briefing room, ever. He guessed that, at a push, it could hold about a hundred and fifty people. Yesterday he had discovered that it was the smallest canteen, ever. In fact, some facet of a distant memory recognised that it had the intimacy of a restaurant. This he hadn't dwelt overmuch on; having not eaten in over twelve hours he'd simply got the chow down his neck. What stopped him in his tracks, and he did think over, was entering a three-man cabin. Of course, he'd heard vague rumours of such things as three-man cabins. It was 'alleged' that very senior officers - senior as in: when these hombres looked troubled whole battle groups shat themselves - were appointed such lavish accommodations. Yet it was still a shock to come face to face with the actual reality.

The day of weirdness had taken an even weirder turn, so he made a speculative punt - him, Rafiu and who else? As he was about to pat himself on the back for his calm response to such unconscionable squandering of *space*, he spotted an occasional table over to one side. Not just any occasional table but one with a glass jug containing what looked like water and several glasses set on it. He'd simply stood rooted to the spot for several seconds, staring at the inappropriateness of all this. Then he figured that this must be part of some bizarre sort of test. Because even on the most sumptuous of luxury civilian yacht a lidless container would be folly. There are some things you definitely do not want floating about should the artificial gravity fail and foremost among them were liquids.

If it was a test, he didn't give a flying frig about its purpose: he'd taken part in too many drills and been on too many ships that had been hit to let this go. He went over and took a sip that confirmed it was plain old water then, from his medikit, jerry rigged and tested for efficacy a watertight lid for the jug. Also, only a lobotomised retard would leave something like glass lying about. He stashed, as well-cushioned as he was able to, the jug and glasses before moving onto other matters. Matters like, first come first serve; he made the top bunk his. Only then had he attended to his ablutions…

Spotting Rafiu he headed across the rapidly filling briefing room and plonked himself down next to the man. As soon as he sat, without looking at each other, both of them started grinning idiotically - nothing needed to be said! *Thorough.* An expression appropriated from the NCOs of basic infantry training. 'Again and be *thorough*!' being balled into your ear by someone who had just upended you best attempt at making a bed. 'Drop and give me fifty. Next time be *thorough*!' All because an errant strand of hair had the impertinence to alight on your tunic during one of the thrice-a-day inspections. Yet the humble grunts had stoically taken the abuses and applied 'thorough' to a very specific situation.

'We who are about to die salute you.' An expression he'd been taught and from what he could hazily recall had something to do with Earth's history. On joining the military one quickly learned that the ditty was utter drivel. What 'we who are about to die' do is have as much sex as the constraints of being on a combat vessel made possible. Fleeting, awkward, frantic, opportunistic sex: after all, this could be literally the very last time. So, when was the last time he'd spent three uninterrupted hours in a darkened cubbyhole of a storeroom with a woman? He had no recollection of any encounter remotely like that but if there had been one it would have been back on Trolus - a remote past life and as such didn't count.

For the infantry, the gold standard for a sexual encounter was 'a *thorough* seeing to' or 'a *thorough* rinsing out' depending on gender and/or partialities. Nobody cared how the matlows quantified anything, sexual or otherwise, because, without exception, they were all unhinged. Now he and Rafiu sat there smirking and doing their damnedest to resist the urge to jump up and dance joyously around the briefing room. From the corner of his eyes he recognised Cropped sinking into the seat on the other side of Rafiu. Then someone sat next to him and in crossing their legs slightly brushed their foot against his calf - nothing as indiscreet as holding hands.

Cropped leant across Rafiu. "Hi, I'm Elspeth," she beamingly introduced herself.

"Bataa." He beamed back.

Rubbing shoulders and softly placing a hand in his lap Blondie lent to Rafiu. "And I'm Lara-Tilly."

"A pleasure to meet you Lara-Tilly," he took her hand and kissed it. "I'm Rafiu."

You would have thought that at some point during the marathon session, while gleaning oodles of intimate details about each other, they would have got around to names, wouldn't you? So, Lara-Tilly it is. As if he wasn't giddy enough; was it is imagination or had the women introduced themselves in a girlfriend-like manner? A gently agitated double-tap elbow in the ribs from Rafiu confirmed his suspicion.

"Room, attention!" somebody shouted and all seated shot to their feet.

A Dandy very similar to The Quartermaster in demeanour and stature but with a Colonel's rank strolled into the room and went up to the front and stood on a small podium. "At ease, please be seated." He waited the few moments it took the assembled to sit and settle down then smiled thinly. "I am The Armourer and I welcome you into the brotherhood of Guardsman." An unspoken current of dissent whisked around the briefing room and his smile widened. "I know, I know, you didn't sign up for this." He paused to unhurriedly survey the faces staring up at him before continuing, "Truth be told if you were the volunteering kind you wouldn't be here. In fact, you're here because you being here, at all, is statistically improbable. Ha, but first some background.

"As veterans of countless engagements you have no doubt, from time to time, questioned why we keep sending the meat into the grinder. Rumour control would have said it's because of the Bulges' miraculous ability to dial-into electric currents. But surely, you would have reasoned, we must have the ability to build battle robots with minimum electric circuitry. The same minimum circuitry we use in your combat suits. And we certainly do have that capability... So why keep serving up the meat?

"Well, long before running into the Bulges, but after we'd developed superlight travel and started spreading out from Earth, some began to suspect that there was a glass ceiling that we were beginning to bang our heads against. There had been a universal assumption that the pursuit of science would eventually present us with a complete understanding of material reality. But material reality was proving to be fiendishly fickle. A minority of scientist, in dark corners well hidden from ridicule, began to postulate that if the answers to some of the fundamental material reality questions weren't to be found in the physical then, by the process of deductive elimination, they must be present in metaphysical.

"Metaphysical: have you ever been head down concentrating on something and for no particular reason stopped, looked up, looked around and stared right into the eyes of someone looking straight at you? The mathematics against that happening by chance is staggering. Yet it has happened to you; it's a common enough human experience that's written off as 'coincidence'. This is where the battle-robots come in, or rather, don't come in. Yes, we have built robots with awesome capabilities, but they always lack one critical element - instincts. You know; when all the info says go right but something in your gut tells you to go left, so you do. Instincts, something beyond algorithms, that we've now learnt is crucial to success in warfare. Hence a Hopper is flown by an AI but a Ground Support Fighter has meat, despite its limitations, in the driving seat.

"OK then, so why not plug the meat directly into that robot with the awesome capabilities - a cyborg? Hands up if you think you know the answer to this question: give a man the power of a god, how long does it take before he starts behaving like a god?" The Armorer scanned the room. "I'd been disappointed if any of you raised a hand, but the answer is measured in seconds. Some of you were on the Merrs 12 shout: pinned down in a chlorine atmosphere for three weeks… If the meat can do a whole three weeks in a combat suit, then it can wear one indefinitely. And when the meat is wearing a combat suit he's pretty godlike, isn't he?" Again, he paused to scan the room. "Anyone here think of themselves as superhuman?" He started grinning again. "You know all those post-ops suit drills you do - totally unnecessary! But they ensure the meat doesn't anthropomorphise with the suit - it's a machine that you 'don' and when you're finished you 'doff'.

"But, militarily, cyborgs are a very attractive idea - human metaphysical instincts married to awesome physical capabilities. If only we could negate the meat's propensity to slide into megalomania because we can build robots that are indistinguishable from people..." He paused then chuckled to himself and that, in itself, was pretty scary. "I sense an element of disbelief. Some of you no doubt consider that there are certain indefinable qualities that make us human that no mere machine could possibly replicate?" He chuckled again. "Anyway, one day some bright spark pointed out that there were ways of wiring the meat other than physically.

"And this is where you, the statistically improbable, come in. You all went through basic infantry training without sustaining serious injury. Whatever your service or specialisation, you hadn't needed reconstructive surgery by the time you reported to your combat units. You made it on to our 'watch list' when you returned from your fourth combat mission without a scratch. And we've had an eye on you ever since. Now you've been on countless missions and yet you still have all your parts. If we were to go with the metaphysical explanation, we wouldn't say you were the statistically improbable, we'd say that you were exceedingly lucky - and you are."

The Armourer stopped, folded his arms, and looked up to the ceiling. Sensing that this was him theatrically giving his audience the opportunity to guess what was coming next Bataa had a valiant stab at it and drew a complete blank.

"*If* one were to start building combat cyborgs the place to kick off would be to harvest the grey matter of the meat with the longest lucky streaks - that would simply be common-sense, wouldn't it?"

Metaphysical or not, the tension in the tiny briefing room abruptly increased alarmingly, teetering on the edge of unbridled violence. This time The Armourer laughed out loud before continuing in an amused tone. "Come now, let's not forget our old friend the megalomaniac deity. It might be undesirable to have the meat wired but if we could somehow get the meat 'connected' to the awesome physical capabilities, that would be cool, wouldn't it? Now, as I'm sure you know, the most basic military unit is the three-man team. So how does this sound; the meat with the longest lucky streaks bonded to two awesome physically capable robots?"

Pulling a frown while looking around the room, The Armourer then sadly shook his head. "No, doesn't float your boat? It's the lack of a 'connection', isn't it? Because a robot is a robot, right? I did say that, had we a mind to, we could build robots that are impossible to tell apart from the meat: identical, right up to the point where we hit the metaphysical glass ceiling, to a living breathing soul... Take a moment to consider what I've just told you."

As The Armourer calmly paced around the podium as if practicing measured dance steps Bataa figured that he didn't need a moment, he flatly disbelieved it and was pretty sure most present did as well. The Armourer ceased his steps and smiled wickedly. "What exactly is a Guardsman? He is the bonded meat in the cyborg sandwich... Room attention!" Slowly, dubiously everyone stood then he continued, "They say the eyes are the windows to the soul and it appears that there's a metaphysical element of truth in this because we've all looked into the eyes of fallen comrades and *known* they've passed. Plus, try as they might, our cyborgneticist have been unable to crack lifelike eyes. Shades off!"

Why all the melodrama? Grinding his teeth, he took off his sunglasses, officers are supposed to give orders without... Lara-Tilly was looking up at him... Holy fuck!! Leaping backwards he bounced off Rafiu, who was having exactly the same repellent reaction, and careered back into her - she easily caught and steadied him. Open mouthed he stood there staring into the blue but lifeless eyes of a… robot!

The voice of The Armourer, now openly sniggering, reverberated around the room. "You have been wired, your first mission as a Guardsman is to try and break the connection." Then the man just sauntered out of the room.

***

Sunglasses off, she sat crossed legged at the opposite end of the bunk and with a neutral expression stared back at him through her lifeless eyes. Yet, there was still a soupcon of animalistic attraction permeating between them. Impossible! She's a fucking machine! *Not she, it!* Somehow knowing that *it* was a machine wasn't anywhere near as big an impediment as it ought to have been. It was the way she… *it*, was sitting: provocative without being provocative, a sort of innocent, 'If you were to ask the question you wouldn't be disappointed with the answer', way of sitting.

One saving grace was the knowledge that he wasn't the only one to have had a meltdown. In fact, of the twenty or so inductees, he had been one of the more composed and, taking a much needed ego boost when it was on offer, considerably more composed than Rafiu. The marine clomped around while cursing, like there was no tomorrow, in some Earth language Bataa didn't recognise. Elspeth… the robot called Elspeth folded its arms and stood patiently like a mother waiting for her child's temper tantrum to run its course…

He had to snap out of this. All he had to do was think and feel *that the robot was just that, a robot. Break the emotional connection!* "Are there any fema… women Guardsmen?"

"Guardsman is an irregular plural and no, there are no women Guardsman... If you are interested, I happen to know that only six percent of inductees ask that as their first breakout questions," she said affably.

"Breakout question?"

"The journey to try severing any emotional attachment to little ole me."

Looking into those blue eyes that were so completely dead that they might as well have been marbles, still… This is ridiculous, she is a machine! Fight it! "Your ergonomics were configured to a template that I would find appealing?"

"No." She gave the slightest shake of her head. "'Template' doesn't really do justice to the multimodal overlapping behaviourisms that make me a tad more than merely appealing; you will love and also, in the paternalistic conjugal sense, care for me. But by all mean go ahead and refuse to give in to it; I won't feel offended you're only obeying orders." She gave him a slight smile.

Stop it! She only smiled! "Why are there no women Guardsman?"

"Women are not as visually sexually stimulated for a start." She uncrossed her legs and rested her head against the bulkhead. "Plus the meta-psychological basis that endows them with the potential to carry to term, then bring a life into being and bond with it means they are also far less predisposed to forming emotional attachments to inanimate objects - even when they do the affinity lacks longevity. And anyway, much more time-consuming enlistment methods, with questionably results, would have to be employed."

"Why would it have to be different - women aren't that different."

"Women are considerably more 'internal'. If we got into a woman's head the way we got into yours, via her knickers, she would probably feel utterly violated and never forgive us. By 'us' I mean the Guardsman Corps."

"But I do feel violated!"

"No, you don't, you feel conned," was said by someone behind him. The voice was so melodious that even without turning he felt that he would probably like its owner. That it came from behind meant she had been standing silent and perfectly still (not particularly difficult if you're a robot, granted) since he'd stormed into the 'three-man cabin' and threw himself onto the bottom bunk.

Also sky blue suited, sunglassesless and dead-eyed she came around to stand in front of him. "I'm Rukshana Thariyan, you have to breakout of *this* as well." Then she did a slow enticing twirl.

The term 'Amerindian' popped into his head; God knows where it came from, but he knew that she looked like one. The darkness of her skin contrasted with her bright white teeth and there was a sexy gap between the front ones. Come to think of it, neither woman was 'perfect' that was probably why they were so attractive… *Get a grip! They are NOT women!*

"Rukshana Thariyan? Is that hyphenated like Lara-Tilly or are devices getting surnames these days?" The moment he'd finished speaking he felt guilty and ashamed… *Get over it! You can't hurt its feelings it's a fucking appliance!*

Locking eyes with him she backed away to sink into a vacant seat. Just from the way she moved he could tell that she'd be the 'naughty' one. "Bataa, it's probably in your best interest to know that we're sentient beings and therefore possess 'free will' so a more precise description would be 'silicone-based life form'. But with that comes a host of thorny legal issues around *rights* that probably won't be addressed until after the Bulges have been dealt with… Or to put it another way, if you want regular quality pussy, you'd betta be nice."

"And charming: Rafiu was so sophisticated and terribly charming," Lara-Tilly chirped in.

He looked into each set of soulless eyes in turn and wondered if there wasn't a little woman hiding somewhere behind each. He gave an involuntary deep sigh before asking, "How many inductees actually mange to 'breakout'?"

"As of today?" Rukshana asked and he nodded. "As of today, none. The Guardsman Corps doesn't invest in the likes of you just to fail. But it is mission critical that your sense of self gets the opportunity to ditch the 'devices' with the wobbly bits and self-lubricating parts because if you're *coerced* into a 'union' with us your balls might retract and your dick shrivel, or some such thing."

"Speaking of which, the magic number is 13.5%. In that we're only 13.5% physically faster, stronger, etc. Apparently, at around 15% female pre-eminence the 'all they really need is a compliant hole with low self-esteem' maleness nosedives into the grumps, leading to testicular retractions and member shrivellings," Lara-Tilly cheerfully added.

He tried really hard not to grin at them, he really did. But he had to concede, he just didn't have any fight left. There is being sexually attracted to a woman. Then there is the quite separate matter of liking a person. Then just to muddy the waters even further there's also being in love with someone. And he was overdosing on all of it. "If you have free will, what sort of things do you like doing?"

Rukshana raised an eyebrow. "Does that mean you've ceded, Sir?"

He shrugged. "You could say that."

"Damn! I was so looking forwards to slinking across the room waving my arse in your general direction."

"I told her you were definitely an arse man." Cupping both her breasts Lara-Tilly stared down at them. "Just think; all this bosomly voluptuousness going to waste."

"I am not an arse man."

Lara-Tilly just looked at him askance and laughed.

"I'm not." He wondered what would make her think that. "I mean I'm into tits as much as the next guy."

"Bataa, you do realise you're arguing the toss with a quantum computing brain, don't you?" Rukshana inquired in an 'I'm simply checking your sanity' tone. "And it should come as no surprise that the kind of things we like doin' is the same kind of things you like doin'."

It took him a while to realise that he was slightly dizzy then it took him a little longer to appreciate why. His recollection of very limited experience of coping with overtly sexual women was that he usually found them overwhelming. And he'd certainly never been in a situation where he had to engage with two: he was being overwhelming overwhelmed. What he needed to do was snap out of this overdosing on oestrogen or its cybernetic analogue and demonstrate that he wasn't a complete dunce. "Are you connected to each other and the ship's AI?"

He'd posed the question to Rukshana but Lara-Tilly lent forward to answer. "Nope. That would lead to a dependency which isn't available in combat. We connect with the ship's AI, each other and you like regular bods, verbally. Can I ask you a question?"

What could she possibly want to know that wasn't already programmed in? "OK."

"Are you gonna to ask him what I think you're gonna ask him?"

"Yep!" Lara-Tilly was now serious, all business. "Bataa, I've searched and searched but nowhere can I find even one teeny weenie secreted subroutine that gives the merest hint I might like girls too."

"Me neither. Not into breasts and not even a suggestion of girlie on girlie. What's occurring?"

"I told you, I like breasts."

"I don't think I heard anybody say you disliked them just that you preferred the arse - don't argue, I could give you your 'handling' stats. But we digress, I know you're from Trolus but surely you must have heard of girl on girl or is it just the boys playing with the boys there?"

They were toying with him and all too effortlessly taking the piss. He needed to assert himself and take the initiative. "Lara-Tilly, what's your surname."

"Heye."

"Did someone choose your names or are you wearing them for a bet?"

She raised an eyebrow then smiled. "I'm particularly fond of both my names so do bear in mind the direct correlation between free will and quality pussy?"

He had to stare off into space for a moment: this was second time in a few minutes that a *robot* was trying to use her pussy to taunt him - twenty-four hours ago, if someone had even suggested such a possibility he'd have dismissed it out-of-hand as beyond stupid. "What happens now?"

"Well, as there'll be no girl on girl, I make myself scarce and you get to know each other." Lara-Tilly slipped off the bunk and, all girly on tip toes, promptly skipped out of the cabin.

***

"Do you know where they've gone?" Rafiu pulled out a chair opposite and, like a man who hadn't had much sleep, slumped into it.

"Dunno. To recharge or whatever? No offence but you looked absolutely fucked."

"Back at you... It's like somebody dipped into my head and pulled out two perfect women who are just up for it."

Well yes, he was feeling a touch 'sore' too. "No, haven't you noticed, they're not perfect, they have lots of little imperfections. For example, Lara-Tilly has a slight lisp that's not very noticeable until you really listen to what she's saying - why would you 'design' that in."

Rafiu pondered this for a long moment. "Hmm, I see what you mean: Ali has this tiny mole-thing beneath her left eye that kind of makes her look sad and, at the same time, really horny." He pondered some more before asking. "How long did your resistance last?"

"Resistance? I wouldn't say there was any resistance, as such. Denial, yes, there was plenty of that and you know what, she just sat there exuding certainty - like a woman who knows she could tip you over the edge by just looking at you in a certain way. I feel so…"

"Feeble?"

"No, not feeble, powerless. Like I have no control over me. God damn it, Rancid Roger profiled us and dared us to defy them."

"Hmm," Rafiu nodded in agreement then after a while asked, "Have you ever been in love?"

"Don't go there! It's lust! They were built so we'd lust after them. It's simply physical proportions, personality traits and programming - you can't be in love with a machine."

Calmly Rafiu looked him over then asked, "Bataa, do you have any idea how hard you're pushing back on that? So hard that…"

"Shut up! Next you'll be saying I'll want them to be having my babies."

"So, the thought has crossed your mind… Face facts, Air Cav, they detailed us down to the last digit and now a couple of automata own our arses."

"Tell me about it." This was the final resignation, and he felt the lifting of a burden and relief at giving in to the inevitable. "Because we care for them, we'll never expose them to unnecessary risks - a prerequisite to operating as a combat team, I suppose."

"Logically we know they're just apparatus but emotionally we'll respond as if they are people - people we care about. Doesn't that make you feel depressingly shallow?"

"Shallow?"

"Yeah, one… well a couple of, thorough seeing tos and they have us bang to rights. That's as shallow as shallow gets; that's shallow as in nothing beneath the surface shallow, *mi compadre*, and it doesn't say much for the male of the species."

"You think so? When was the last time you got a thorough anything?"

"Ahh, I get your drift; can't say I ever have." Pulling a face like he was tasting something particularly pleasurable Rafiu continued, "And I suppose by definition anything thorough has to be deep. That's deep as in touch your very soul, deep."

"Totally... Mind you, I still feel I made it too easy for Rancid Roger - should have been able to hold out for at least a couple of days… Man, we been pussy whipped!"

"That's like bitching about being hit by a man-tracking, body temperature seeking, DNA homing micro missile… What kind of resources went into creating just one of them, do you suppose?"

Stopping to ponder the question Bataa found himself struggling to conceive of a number that made meaningful financial sense. Clearly the answer lay beyond any point of reference in the realm he inhabited. "A shit load and you do realise that they could be spoiling us for real women, don't you?"

"Yeah, buckets upon buckets of shit loads! Just to keep the little boys in the sky-blue smocks happy? I don't think so! Rancid Roger always looks for a serious return on any investment. You're worried about real women? I'd say we'd be lucky if we ever get anywhere near a real woman again."

Bataa felt a chill run down is spine. "In harm's way, in peril: they're gonna drop us in deep, deep do do, aren't they?"

Before Rafiu could respond a Dandy, sporting corporals' stripes came into the canteen and balled out, "Atwali, Bashe, Delzoppo, Hoskins, Qubert and Rashwan you're up! To First Aid."

***

Despite the obvious limitations, their internal body plan was based on a living breathing person. No one explained why but he guessed that it was so that the human component didn't have too much to unlearn. Someone au fait with basic field medicine, and all combat personnel were, could render remedial treatment. Their 'blood', however, was cream coloured so anybody would instantly know that, despite appearances, they weren't dealing with an injured person. Where they physiology really departed from the norm were strategically placed pressure points that could shut off blood flow to specific areas of the body. They wouldn't bleed to death but loss of too much blood led to immobility.

Most of what they had to learn was shown to them on holograms but with the pressure points they practised locating, identifying, and manipulating on a mannequin. Also, of note about the human-like 'chassis' was the inbuilt redundancy - no single central pump (heart) or processing centre (brain). But what was really instructive about this training session though was that nothing was said about how they were powered or actually worked - just standard field medicine but for robots. It was pretty obvious that a first aid closet was the only shipboard cubical equipped to medicate a damaged/injured robot. He was also fairly sure there were secret standing orders to get anybody apparently gushing creamy blood from triage to one PDQ.

Where the instructors were more forthcoming, almost to the point of garrulousness, was answering question they hadn't been asked: "Of course your Little Darlings feel pain." "Sleep no, rest yes - a little downtime never goes amiss." "Why care about what would happen to them if you died, you'd be dead." "The CO is known as The Armourer because your pair of sweethearts are collectively known as your Armour - their raison d'etre is to protect and keep your baby soft skins safe." "Moody? My dear boy, they have female-brain personalities." "Nothing lives for ever but your average human five score and ten is eminently doable for them."

And so on until at some point during this 'medical briefing' Bataa began to get an inkling as to why all the officers, NCO's, and instructors he'd encountered were male. One scenario their loquacity hadn't elucidated was what happens when the Armour do their job and the Guardsman survives but they don't. By the time his group were exiting the cubicle he'd inferred why, despite their obvious vast combat experience, his superiors' behaviour was so laidback and unmilitary. The simple fact was no matter how well a soldier might try to hide it he always felt a sense of loss coupled with guilt over comrades who had fallen; especially those who had been close enough to be considered friends.

The best of the very best not only paid their dues, but they also survived. Because they were the best at surviving, they became the Directing Staff instructors. If the maggots took onboard the DS's words of wisdom, then, they too might survive. But what if only a part of you survived? Yes, you were brothers-in-arms; yes, you may have been very close; yes, you would have put your life on the line for them; *but* you were never in love with your confederates. What magnitude of bereavement trauma resulted in such elevated degrees of accomplished nonchalance as exhibited by the DS? This meant either you could only be bonded to Armour once or these guys were given the choice not to be bonded again. Whichever way it went, here was something to sink his philosophical teeth into…

With suspiciously impeccable timing both Rukshana and Lara-Tilly came strolling down the corridor to halt in front of him. "No rest for the wicked. Now you know which buttons to press we three are off to the battle simulator," Rukshana informed him as each woman pointedly positioned herself either side of him. Because this effectively blocked the corridor he thought it pertinent to point this out, but she pre-empted him, "Hey, did you not hear 'battle simulator'? Your *Armour* is getting its game face on."

As they collectively turned to head for the battle sim, he spotted Rafiu being led off by Elspeth and, he presumed, Ali. Both women were very different: in terms of height, hue, strut and build they were poles apart and yet, at the same time, there was a definitely commonality. Although Bataa couldn't precisely define what it was, Rafiu had a *type*. With regards to Rukshana and Lara-Tilly he wondered if he also had a type because if he did it wasn't blindingly obvious to…

"You haven't asked," Lara-Tilly said in a mildly chiding tone.

He guessed he was being ribbed so he waited several seconds before responding. "What haven't I asked?"

"And I would've thought that it would be first thing you'd want to know," Rukshana joined the tease.

It ought to be really unsurprising that they performed as a slick double act. "I'm so sorry, when are your birthdays?"

"We weren't *born* so how can we have birthdays?" Rukshana retorted dismissively then added, "And you know that's not what we meant."

"Yeah, you should want to know how long a marriage usually last," Lara-Tilly feigned being hurt.

If his 'inner man' was having an adverse reaction to the 'marriage' notion it was doing so remarkably inaudibly. Allowing his mind to drift he mentally replayed an old expression he'd pick up that could only have originated on Earth. No matter if it looks like, walks like and flies like, as far as he was concerned, it still needs to quack… That's why they are not perfect! They also have to break your balls like real women do. "I don't do 'usually'. How long has the longest marriage lasted?"

"Funny that you should ask, they've recently celebrated their bronze wedding anniversary." Lara-Tilly was now all smiles.

"What?"

"You're so provincial, dearest, that's eight years." Rukshana had also lightened up.

Eight years? That's several lifetimes for combat personnel…

"That's exceptional and though our marriages never end in divorce, the norm is about seven months or two combat missions," Rukshana advised as a mere detail.

Never in a month of Sundays would he have expected a robot to display fear or worry but behind the blasé he sensed that there was genuine concern. This was conformed when Lara-Tilly lightly elbowed him in the ribs. "The longevity of our continued existence will all be down to you, so, just how lucky are you Bataa Basche?"

Chapter 3

In all the military drillings and beastings he'd experienced, which were invariably predicated on pushing you to your supposed limits then pushing beyond that, had he ever imagine a scenario where he'd be too tired to have sex with a woman who wanted to have sex with him. Yet here he was with two (providing you weren't overly fussy with definitions) who he was pretty sure would and he was so far past being exhausted that he was starting to hallucinate. It's easy to be certain about hallucinating when an M'Tata, a six-limb reptilian beast native to Trolus, mooches past you in the corridor of a spaceship.

All he wanted was to crawl into his bunk and get some shuteye. But no, they tossed tradition out the window and demoted him to the bottom bunk: 'I'm not climbing all the way up there to give you a blow job'. 'Yeah, and like the moment I start doing anything interesting I'll be banging my head on the ceiling.' He was far too weary to argue and the minuscule bit of his intellect still properly functioning gleefully agreed with them. Getting into the bottom zero-G cocoon he stretched out and banished the outside would by zipping it shut... This was ridiculous his mind, in a particularly fuzzy way, was still buzzing - odd as it seemed, he felt too tired to sleep.

As best as he could recall they had spent the last thirty-six hours, or so, practising moving tactically and covertly either as a tight or dispersed three-man fire team. No enemy, no weapons, no incoming just getting from here to there in a simulated densely foliaged area without being spotted - the stuff you were taught in the first week of basic infantry training. At the outset he'd felt almost insulted to be tasked with such a facile undertaking. And sure enough things started off pretty straightforward enough. Even when they'd moved on to dispersed manoeuvres all appeared to be going along swimmingly.

Each member of a fire team had to have a pretty good idea of where the rest of the team were even when they were out of sight: one just had a sense of where they were and what they were likely to be up to. In all his hundreds of exercises and missions he'd never once stopped to consider how he was able to accomplish this. That was right up to the point where the childishly simple exercises started to come apart at the seams. It was also when he discovered that Armour had fantastically good hearing. Once on the move if either woman could not see or hear where the other team members were in relation to themselves, they seemed incapable of figuring it out or even making an educated guess. This, of course, made it impossible to be on the same page tactically.

Frustration didn't do justice to what he began to feel after nearly twelve hours of this and the DS instructors just let it build until he was right at the point of losing it then they intervened. "Rule One: the first, foremost and singular fundamental concept to keep front-of-mind at all time and in all situations is that although Armour can run multifaceted simultaneous simulations, they have no theory of mind. They can respond with awe-inspiring swiftness, but they cannot, repeat, *cannot*, to make doubly sure, **cannot**, anticipate your actions in a combat situation! There is no Rule Two."

He'd never heard of a 'theory of mind' but he knew what an idiot savant was and he was pretty sure that he'd been saddled with two of them. They learned very fast but couldn't take what they knew and adapt it to an entirely new but 'similar' situation - it was like they always had to go right back to the very beginning with everything. They were completely linear - once they learned a rule, they would follow it slavishly even at the expense of common sense. They couldn't improvise; they couldn't invent; they couldn't go 'seat-of-the-pants'.

Some thirty hours into it while (having factored in their exceptional hearing) fulminating under his breath at being thwarted at every turn by two dull, artless, unimaginative, morons it suddenly came to him. Most of the time, he had a good sense of where they both were - usually in the wrong tactical position for the situation. So, to hang on to his sanity all he needed do was respond to what they were most likely to do as opposed to reacting to what they should do. These drills weren't for them; they were for him to adjust to fighting alongside imbeciles with zero combat nous. To make it work from their perspective he simply needed to be where they would expect him logically to be.

Thirty-six hours of pain but he finally 'got it' - they didn't have instincts! For the three of them to operate as an effective team *he* needed to adjust to their one-dimensional thinking: in a tactical movement exercise the 'best' route to take would be one that offered the best cover and concealment, end. Other, human, goes-without-saying elements such as ease of movement wouldn't be factored in. Also, if he was about to make a move on pure intuition, he either had to inform them or execute it knowing they would be singing from a different hymn sheet. They good news was that they always backed his move instantly without question or hesitation. Once he'd made these psychological adjustments the ridiculously easy exercise became ridiculously easy...

***

They weren't yet playing in combat suits, but they were now fully occupied in exercises involving projectile weapons with dummy rounds. The DS had also steadily ramped-up the difficulty of the round-the-clock beastings only letting up so that the Sap could push some Z's (about three uninterrupted hours if he was extremely lucky). Yet, as a fire team they were getting there, and he was learning. The Armour weren't total cretins, he didn't have to do their thinking for them, and they were phenomenally good at dealing with the immediate or the obvious. In these situations, they were the best combat soldiers he'd ever worked alongside: limiting his role to merely trying to keep up with them. Where they fell down and fell down badly was in anticipating what was likely to be coming over the horizon or out of the left field. This was when he came into his own: if time allowed he gave them a 'heads-up', if it didn't he went solo and dealt with whatever it was; in the full knowledge that 'eventually' they'd catch on and tune in …

It was the smell that nudged him out of his reverie causing him to look up: coffee - that foul-tasting concoction produced on Earth. The Armourer pulled out a chair opposite him and languidly sank into it before he could stand to attention. In his hand was a mug with steam slowly rising, he then waved the lidless receptacle in his general direction banishing any formality between them. "As you've nearly completed your training, it's time I bring you up to speed on where we stand in the Order of Battle."

Bataa kept chewing his breakfast and simply stared at the container, the contents obviously very hot; what if the artificial gravity cut out just then?

"Unlike other special forces, us and the Stingers operate completely autonomously: within the fleet but outside the normal command and control channels. The Stingers are the solo operators optimised for covert aggressor missions such as insertion assault, sabotage, or interdiction. Guardsman operations, on the other hand, are long-term deep penetration; reconnaissance, pathfinder, cartography, and the like - a battlegroup's clandestine senses. Not the mission for one person as you can see but ideal for a small tightknit team; it means that if you find you're shooting at something then the mission has probably gone tits-up."

The Armourer paused as if to give him the opportunity to ask a question but Bataa kept his lips buttoned.

"I'm sure you've noted that we are on deck 12B and I'm equally sure you've never seen a ship's schematic with a B deck. Most destroyers and larger ships have a self-contained concealed B deck that's sanitised from the rest of the vessel where a Guardsman detachment of up to six infiltration-teams hang out. As we can't really intermingle and partake of the usual shipborne diversions, B decks tend to be shamelessly more spaciously appointed." The Armourer took a sip from is mug, another invitation for a question.

Bataa thought he'd chance his arm. "Where is your Armour, Sir?"

The Armourer smiled and although Bataa couldn't see past his sunglass he knew his eyes were sparkling. "That's a good question. Rukshana and Lara-Tilly can be considered to be third generation Armour - not only in a developmental sense but also in a deployment sense... Desperate and backs against the wall, about eleven years ago, as soon as the first generation were created they were teamed - not necessarily in a sexual but certainly in an intimate relationship sense - with Stingers and deployed. It wasn't too long before it became pretty evident that Stingers viewed Armour as resources to be employed and discarded as needed; why would they show empathy to a machine when they didn't do it to flesh. It wasn't all a total waste, mind; the powers-that-be got invaluable insight into how Stingers behaved in relationships and from that point started pairing them off with a non-combatant *Sponge* - not another automaton but a more cost effective human who actually got off on soaking-up some of a Stinger's 'dark psychic energy'. The idea being that this made them slightly more compliant and controllable."

He caught himself forming the thought, '*Hyperbole*' and shunted it back to wherever it was emerging from because if a month ago someone had told him about sex-on-legs Goddess androids he'd have thought hyperbole then too.

"With the Stingers lessoned learned the Guardsman Corps was formed and the second generation, my generation, of Armour were attuned so perfectly to us and our needs that we would never consider sacrificing them. We were then dropped in as elite heavy fire teams up at the sharp end with the Stingers… And we were pretty damn effective, if I say so myself. So effective that it took several years for the enervating brain-training the Guardsman were undergoing to become apparent: butt-clenchingly terrifying, erratic warfare against an unfathomable enemy immediately followed by debauched, scrumptious, wish-fulfilling overindulgences immediately followed by butt-clenchingly, terrifying erratic warfare, etc. etc."

"Not only had our fear and reward centres become scrambled they were being incessantly, repetitiously and sequentially maxed out. You've no doubt come across folks who had copped a large dose of the flak happies; well, that's not even on the first rung when compared to where we were at." He paused momentarily to sadly look down into is mug. "Ninety-four percent of second-generation Armour died because their hyper-gung-ho Guardsman had lost the plot and all perspective on boundaries and the possible."

Bataa realised his mouth had sagged open. The Armourer took another sip then smiled wistfully. "Those few of us who outlived our Armour took our guilt-ridden cold turkey on the chin and, like any ex-addict, have to abstain from the 'drug' for good. That lesson has been learnt; now the Stingers have the sharp end all to themselves and you'll enjoy being with your Armour, but they'll ensure you'll never get hooked on them…"

Batta suddenly felt uncomfortable. "But I think I may already be hooked, Sir."

"You're smitten, as you should be, but I very much doubt you're hooked." The Armourer smiled paternally at him. "Basche, your profile shows that you have a fairly unsophisticated attitude towards sex - transactional in nature thus all that's required is permission or denial; a simply 'yes' or a simple 'no'. Lara-Tilly and Rukshana have *reciprocal* transactional temperaments as part of their emotional make-up so that's your piece of heaven. But remember, 'The same key that lets you into heaven can open every door in hell'… you have worked out that they do have real emotions, haven't you?"

Yes, he had, and it was alright for them to tease him about not being a tits man but what's this bollocksology about unsophisticated sex? "If a woman does not explicitly give her consent to having sex then that's rape, Sir."

Again, The Armourer smiled. "Quite right, Basche, quite right." He stopped as if leaving it at that, pondered for a moment and then continued, "However, there are other universes out there: the realm of 'maybe', or of eroticism, or of conquest, or of seduction, or of submission and so many, many more. They are your type of girls, but you're not hooked." He reached into his top pocket and pulled out a data crystal. "This is your pre-deployment briefing, and you have twenty-four hours to get totally up to speed. A Guardsman has the authority to issue verbal commands to various automatics, commandeer vessels, take command of various units, and call upon a host of fleet resources as they see fit. This outlines how and where the limits of your empowerment lie." He handed across the crystal. "Tomorrow you, without your gals as they already have it programmed in, will be put through various directing simulations and after you've attained the required standard, report to The Quartermaster for your new suit."

As Bataa took the crystal in one hand The Armourer put down his mug, reached across, took his other hand and with a genuine smile, shook it.

***

Anybody who knows anything about combat suits knows that the most important thing was to get the boots fitting comfortably first. The human ankle was one of the few remaining areas where Nature's engineers still outperformed their human counterparts. Slim yet robust enough to carry the total body weight while flexible enough to enable the foot to pivot. Even Rukshana and Lara-Tilly were a bit heavy-set around theirs. Combat boots were 'thick with elephantiasis' around the ankles causing their wearers to walk with a wider gate than they would normally - just one of the many adjustments one had to make when wearing a suit. Then there was the fit of the actual foot part. Even in powered combat suits Grunts still made their living from yomping so ill-fitting footwear would still ruin your day.

He was all set for a long session of being particular and pedantic about the fitting of his boots but as soon as he walked into the 'stores' The Quartermaster looked up from the screen he was scrutinising, nodded him over to a pair of suit boots and said, "Saddle up."

Bataa wasn't familiar with the expression but guessed it meant to try them on so he we went over to do as instructed. That only the boots were present testified to the fact that The Quartermaster knew his stuff. Suites were custom tailored from body moulds and laser scans and so in theory should be a perfect fit. The reality was that they never fitted properly and took ages to get just right. And you really did want them fitting just right: anything that could accelerate from zero to thirty k.p.h. in under two seconds could do serious damage if the fit wasn't completely skin-tight. When he kicked off his ship boots with their built-in emergency maglock and stepped into the suit boot the general feeling of yet even more weirdness began to percolate up from somewhere. He stepped into the other boot, the pair auto locked, and as he took a couple of paces the feeling of weirdness came back with a vengeance - it took weeks to dial-in a new pair of boots yet this pair felt like he'd had them for months.

The Quartermaster knowingly smirked over at him. "Snug? The rest is round the back, slip it on then you can wear it out."

The master sergeant statement indicated total confidence that the suit would need no fine-tuning and Bataa's experience with the boots lent some justification to that confidence, still… "How were you able to…?"

"Despite appearances to the contrary we've owned your arse for the last seven months, now go try on the rest."

Was he becoming accustomed to the informality with which a Guardsman issued commands? Approaching the footless suit hanging on a mini rack he started scrutinising it in the full knowledge that he would need to become intimately familiar with it. Yes, it looked a bit like a Stingers, but it was now obvious that this was more a concealment suit rather that a combat suit. Yes, it was mirror shiny but its surface also had adaptive camouflage and EM vary-spectra invisibility - if he hadn't been so overawed with the fitting of the boots he would've already clued in it was made from the same material.

All shipborne infantry was expected to 'suit & boot' in under five minutes. Factoring in his unfamiliarity with the suit but being already 'boots on' he estimated that it took him a respectable two hundred and ten seconds. However, it was as he went through the standard system checks that his new suit really revealed itself to him: survivability over manoeuvrability, stealth over speed, endurance over fire power - definitely designed and optimised for Recon. Its thermal range was also impressive; a standard combat suit couldn't function at minus two hundred and two degrees Celsius. But it was it operating up at seven hundred degrees C that was extraordinary - the standard suit's upper limit was just above the melting point of lead at three hundred and fifty degrees C.

The suits operating parameters screamed rocky planets or moons with atmospheres seriously inimical to human life - oh deep joy! Also, a combat suit couldn't be perfectly insulated, or the occupant would slowly stew; Saps were exothermic creatures after all. So how did it manage to dump this generated heat when the 'outside' temperature was so much hotter? Cycling through the various menus and diagnostic Bataa couldn't discover an answer but he was pretty sure that he was suited in something exceptional, expensive and, low and behold, a *perfect* fit.

He strolled up to The Quartermaster with the helmeted suit walking along, stride for stride, closely behind him like an overly diligent bodyguard. As the only one in his brigade who could pull off such shenanigans, gleefully he anticipated the man's reaction. The Quartermaster didn't even bat an eyelid and Bataa instantly felt foolish. Clearly the Dandy had seen this stunt before, perhaps many times. Plus, he'd been on their radar since his fourth mission so they probably knew about his party trick of hotwiring and running zombie suits.

"As soon as you leave here grab your kit and caboodle and make your way to Bay 12B, you're being posted." The Quartermaster stuck out his hand.

He was too stunned to respond and simply stared at the offered hand. They were far from mission ready. "What about suit-on manoeuvres?"

"The crucial precept that Armour doesn't operate on intuition is now engraved into your brain so you're ready as you'll ever be." Without any embarrassment he kept his hand extended and gave him a wry smile. "Look after your girls and they'll look after you."

Still not a hundred percent convinced, and with the suit mirroring the motion, he took The Quartermaster's proffered hand and shook it. Turning, he started strolling out endeavouring to move with the same graceful aplomb Dandies did…

"Walk like that and you'll have every limp-wristed matlow from here to Earth sniffing around you; lean back, relax your shoulders," was the amused advice that trailed the zombie suit out of the stores. And who was standing there with their acute hearing?

"No girl on girl and a nascent matlow magnet, makes you wonder, doesn't it?" Rukshana's opening remark was uttered straight-faced as if thinking aloud.

"Trolus' is a polyandrous culture as I understand it, so what do the boys do to amuse themselves when the girl isn't around, I wonder?" Lara-Tilly seemed to be having a moment of her own.

He let all this slide because both of them had a rucksack on, a zombie suit standing behind them and Lara-Tilly had his rucksack in an embrace. He tried and failed to hold back the feeling of dejection at his zombie suit trick not being exceptional or a big deal. "We have to go to Bay 12B, we're being posted," he informed them trying to sound sombre.

"We know, so do lead on, oh, Lord and Master." Lara-Tilly then theatrically scuttled out of his way.

Setting off it occurred to him that neither of them had ever been on a combat mission so the inappropriateness of this humour at this time was probably totally lost on them. These could be their last moments of piece and tranquillity and really ought to be a time of reflection...

"A Guardsman does not *mince*!" Rukshana quietly hissed.

Lara-Tilly started looking around wildly. "How embarrassing! Do you think anybody we know has seen us?"

Rukshana brushed past him. "Like this, lover boy." Prancing ahead even her tagging along zombie suit managed to move with a certain panache.

"Follow!" Lara-Tilly gave him a gentle shove in the back. "He might not be crazy about breasts, but a girl can't have the world thinking her man's light on his feet."

She gave him firmer push before he got with the programme; syncing with Rukshana's motion but toning down the curvy feminine wiggle, he heeded The Quartermaster's advice; easing back he relaxed his shoulders and attempted to 'stroll'.

"That's my boy." Slapping him hard on the arse, Lara-Tilly then added, "Shades on, glide when you move, walk with a swagger."

Rukshana dropped back to be beside him. "Splendidly cool as fuck!"

Really, really difficult to be solemn with them around... Ahead, he spotted a very aggravated looking Rafiu with Elspeth and Ali, visibly giving him space, in tow. The trio had no doubt just exited the battle sim. Both pairs of women immediately came to a halt leaving him and Rafiu to close the distance between them to get some privacy. With their hearing abilities was it really that private? If Armour couldn't intuit, how were they able to figure out that privacy was what was needed? Stupid, it wasn't that complicated, they'd worked it out.

It had been a couple of days since he'd last seen Rafiu and nearly a week since they'd had a proper conversation. He knew that his fire team integration with his Armour had progressed more rapidly than Rafiu's. When talking through various scenarios it became obvious that this was not because he was a more proficient soldier but because he'd jacked into his girls much faster. Rafiu was finding Ali and Elspeth's actions in combat situations aberrant and totally erratic, whereas he found Lara-Tilly and Rukshana's predictably dim-witted. Who knows, this might be where an unsophisticated attitude to sex comes in.

"Head down, arse flat, hug the ground."

"In the marines we say, 'Glorious death; die cursing, die firing.'"

Chapter 4

They were intercepted en route to Bay 12B by a corporal who unceremoniously handed over a silver foil that solely contained the name of the ship they were to report to. Bataa now understood that B decks only had palm readers because retina scans left Armour at a distinct disadvantage. Contrary to his own expectations it now appeared that he'd adjusted to this Dandy lark, after all Air Cav were nothing if not flexible. Without being told, he also understood that in any situation that necessitated the removal of sunglasses, such as an obligatory retina scan, he needed to step forward pretty damn smartish to ensure they kept theirs on at all costs. OK, so why didn't their orders tell him which Bay to report to?

"Destination *Pantheon*, launch when cleared." Revelling in giving instructions to an automatic he was still taken by surprise at the Hopper's prompt response.

"*Destination* Pantheon. *Clearance received. Launching.*"

"I do so like it when he's being all masterful, don't you?" Rukshana crossed her legs and beamed at him while Lara-Tilly nodded exaggeratedly in agreement.

Was this a consequence of no longer being relentlessly drilled? Had either of them developed strategies to cope with idle time? He thought he saw a way of bringing this nonsense to an end. "Have you ever left this ship?

"Well, yes and no... We became fully conscious here, but I doubt we were created in space, Gorgeous," Lara-Tilly breathlessly informed him.

"And how long have you been awake?"

"When it was confirmed that you'd made it off Omega Zero Three in one piece - so about three and a half weeks. While we're on the subject of being awake, would you like a blow job?" Rukshana fluttered her eyelids.

For some reason he'd been expecting an answer measured in months, several months. What would have been done with them if he hadn't made it? Reconfigured? Reprogrammed? He doubted they would know the answer... Damnit! He'd missed the Hopper exiting into space, something he had been really looking forward to. Would he ever get used to being with these two…?

"That can't be normal," Lara-Tilly muttered full of disappointment.

"Or natural, I'd say," Rukshana agreed.

Had he missed something? "What can't be?"

Turning her back on him Rukshana, folded her arms under her bosoms and started pouting. Looking wounded Lara-Tilly squared up to him. "So, are you saying you'd prefer one from another man?"

They'd been posted to gods knows where which meant they'll be up to their eyes in gods knows what for only gods knows how long… Their personalities were programmed to be attuned to his so what did this continuous piss-taking reveal about him? That he liked a woman with a sharp wit …? More importantly could this total absence of inquisitiveness about the future be linked to their lack of instincts? "Do you have any knowledge or insight on how long our posting on *Pantheon* is likely to last?"

"It's an art form and I'm *really* good at it!" Rukshana wailed.

"Me too. Most 'heterosexual' men would give their right arm to be with us."

"It's OK to say you don't know if you don't know." He needed to bring some sombreness to the situation, right now. "As for blow jobs, there's a time and place for everything and at this precise moment I'm scared shitless. In the Air Cav I might not have known the exact mission, but I always knew what was expected of me."

Rukshana, in her naughty guise, bounced out of her seat, loped over and stood imposingly in front of him. "And because the expectations on us are very precise, to keep you alive and happy, we can see you're fretting so get your dick out so we can relieve some of that stress."

How can a robot understand humour but have no intuition? "Will you two please stop this I have lots to get my brain around, like…

"And why, exactly, should that stop me getting my lips round something else?"

"I mean it, stop… Hang on a sec, this deep mirth is all front, isn't it? It's how you deal with fear or worry, right?"

Rukshana smiled, turned, and went back to sit in her seat. "We're programmed to be combat brave so, no, it's not fear."

"The quantum computing brain doesn't do uncertainty well," Lara-Tilly articulated.

"Are you saying that all this 'come on big boy' behaviour is going to be your nervous tic?"

Pulling a puzzled frown Lara-Tilly turned to Rukshana. "Did you ever use the word 'big' in that regards because I certainly didn't?"

"I have no idea where he got the notion that that could, by any stretch of the imagination, be considered 'big'. Moderately sufficient, I'd say."

"Passably adequate," Lara-Tilly concurred.

Though no cyborgneticist he thought he'd challenge himself to see if he could take a mental leap and string this together in a logical fashion: their brains were simply very smart programs so; their minds couldn't move outside that programming, can't *wander* so; they can't drift off into day dreams so; when they didn't have specific tasks to perform they reverted to their base programming… Shit! This was his mother… Whenever either of his dads got grumpy, she invariably started gently teasing them and kept at it until they lightened-up. Was this coincidence or could Rancid Roger dig that deep…? Either way, a most disturbing revelation!

"Uncertainty is my middle name so why don't you let me carry that particular load. Liberating the quantum computing brains to indulge in the things quantum computing brains ought to be good at indulging in."

Rukshana raised an eyebrow. "Things? Such as?"

Reflecting that they had genuine emotions, female-brain emotions, he suppressed a smile. "Oh, I dunno, things like brewing up the next sex session so that it's an even bigger blast than the last."

Lara-Tilly sat up fully alert. "Is anything off the table in terms of invention or experimentation?"

"You call it, I'll be game."

"Both women looked at each and starting grinning from ear to ear then Rukshana glanced at him. "My boy, do you know what you've let yourself in for?"

Logical thinkers who had the same aptitude for prognostication as did a lump of wood. "I most certainly do, not just anything that's physically possible but a 'blast' - must be pleasurable to all concerned."

"Damn! You're not just a pretty face, are you?" Lara-Tilly looked genuinely surprised.

"Don't you mind him, girl. I've dreamt-up enough to last months without even trying and that's not including the three of us in the same bunk at the same time."

"*Arrival* Pantheon. *Disembark.*"

Hard to believe they'd distracted him to the point of him not even noticing entering the Bay and the Hopper landing… But of course, that was exactly what they were doing, distracting him. Having been so wrapped up in anticipating and compensating for their idiotic tactical performance he'd never once considered how they might have dialled-in to him. While they gathered their kit and zombie suits to exit the craft he casually asked, "Can you really tell when I'm worried?"

Leading the way Rukshana chirped up, "Concerned, perturbed, worried, frightened, terrified, wetted ya pants, spurted brown adrenalin."

The huge, stencilled numbers along the wall said, 'Bay 27'. Enormous Bay, high Bay number - so a really big ship then. Why hadn't they arrived in Bay 27B…?

"Hug, snog, hand job, tit wank, blow job, balls deep, donkey punch," Lara-Tilly cheerfully provided the addendum to Rukshana's itemisation.

He didn't suppose it would lessen their witticisms if he asked what a donkey punch was. "Can I ask you to be less… flippant at times when you see me… preoccupied?"

"That would be a touch difficult. That's unless you want us to have complete personality bypasses as it's all hardwired. And you wouldn't want just two ole dreary automatons with you, would you?" Lara-Tilly stated matter-of-factly.

"Deflection! In all the history of mankind how often has a man cried off a blow job from buxom gorgeousnesses the likes of us, do ya think?" Rukshana made a general enquiry to no one in particular.

He must have been seriously distracted because he hadn't noticed the Dandy, a Lieutenant, approaching until he was standing in front of them. Reflexively he started the motion but instinctively knew he ought not to salute, it wasn't the Guardsman way. The Lieutenant - about his age, Asiatic, much shorter and skinny - made a slight formal bow to Lara-Tilly and Rukshana. "Ladies." Then he stepped up to him and took his hand in a firm handshake. "Welcome, brother."

Brother? The marines had some weird camaraderie shit but even they weren't this touchy-feely. If you attempted any of this in the Air Cav, you'd have someone stuffing their fist down your throat.

"My name is Malachi. Leave your kit here and accompany me," he said pleasantly enough.

Accompany him where? Easy-going Guardsman or not, the guy was still a Lieutenant so Bataa thought it best not to ask. Malachi waited patiently as the women deactivated the zombie suits then turned, and with a nod, invited Bataa to join him and, with the women trailing, headed for the Bay exit. "You're not being posted to *Pantheon*, you're here for a briefing."

As soon as they exited the Bay Bataa could instinctively tell that this ship wasn't as stuffed with the multitudes as most, so not a carrier then. Even so the evil glares were on them before the Bay doors had closed. He lent back, relaxed his shoulders and side by side with Malachi ignored it all. Just as he started 'strutting his stuff' he was struck by a cascade of blinding insights. Firstly, he now suddenly *understood* why so much of his education had been about Earth: Earth this, Earth that, this on Earth, that on Earth. Earth, a planet he was unlikely to ever visit even if he lived several lifetimes.

Now he got it - communication. Communication wasn't only about language; there were also the essential elements such as metaphors, symbolisms, allegories, euphemisms, idioms. Someone from Ningu, a planet that was on the ragged edge of borderline Earth-like and therefore barely habitable, spoke the same language as someone from Ebury, a planet that was Earth-like to the extent that its population was over a billion. Yet, Standard English could only take you so far; one needed to be able to pull the most apposite rabbit out of the hat (when did he learn what a rabbit was?) to convey one's thoughts and ideas.

This led to the second insight: a Guardsman wasn't a Dandy after all. He was a *peacock* whose primary function was to draw attention from the peahens. Reflecting for a moment, Bataa couldn't recall a single instance where the urge to just walk up to one and punch their lights out was directed at a female Guardsman. So, alongside Malachi he strutted with even more smugness.

His inflated sense of smugness started to rapidly evaporate as they approached the guards posted at the entrance of OpsCen. During an operation over a year ago Bataa had once hand-delivered personal non-electrical comms to a field command but an OpsCen was just that; the nerve centre of a naval battle group - very rarefied air indeed. He was almost on the point of faltering when Lara-Tilly or Rukshana (he didn't turn to see which one) moved up and gently bumped him back onto the path of the super cool.

No rigmarole, no formalities, the guards acknowledged their presence with a nod, and they were allowed to enter OpsCen... It was a circular Jump Suite! Why was he so surprised? He supposed that it was possible to configure a Jump Suite to any arrangement one liked, he'd just never heard of or seen a circular one before. As he was getting over the odd shape of the Suite, he clued in to the seating arrangements. Six concentric rings of seats faced an inner ring of eight seats that faced outward; the seats furthest from the centre were against the Suite's wall. Although there were only about ten people present, in this area that could probably accommodate an infantry company, there was no doubt about where the power lay here. And, yet another surprise, there she sat, Admiral of the Fleet Akobundu-Tan.

The last he'd heard she was all the way back on Earth receiving a hero's welcome over of the Omega Zero Three jamboree. He'd thought she'd been particularly impressive because after being decorated and conspicuously feted, the first opportunity she got to speak, she praised, 'The dedication, professionalism and unwavering courage of every man and woman under her command'. Yet here she was back on the case; even more impressive. With very dark skin and also epicanthic folds in her eyes she could easily have been Rafiu's mother except she was *tiny*. Because he was two point two metres tall he tended to think of most women as small: he would have gone as far as saying that Lara-Tilly was petite but it was now obvious that the Admiral was the epitome of petite.

Petite but exuding bucket loads of sub-zero 'don't fuck with me' cool - it wouldn't have surprised him in the least to discover that the Guardsman had been modelled on her. Sitting to her immediate left he recognised Field Martial Hooper. The word 'round the fleet was that he'd actually freelanced on the Omega Zero Three gig and had personally led a couple of assaults against Bulge mounds. Bataa was inclined to accept this version of events because it would imply that the General was 'Airborne'. Having a land forces commander that was 'Airborne', as opposed to the Airborne Calvary, gave credence as to why *this* planetary assault had been executed in such a gung-ho - drop in unannounced, fuck 'em hard up the arse, lift out - fashion. Marines and the regular infantry tended to require the flattening of everything first, before going in.

There were a couple of Staff Officers sitting with them, but Malachi led their party, through a constellation of holograms projected in the air, to halt before the commanders and, as the officer, saluted. Both Admiral and Field Martial nodded in acknowledgement then concurrent with the Field Martial gesticulating for them to sit the inner circle of inward facing seats rotated so that four empty seats faced the commanders - amazing, the rotating seats easily topped his zombie suit party piece. Wasn't it considered rude and insubordinate to sit in the presence of such senior officers? Then again, hadn't they just received a nonverbal command to sit?

Malachi and the women immediately sat and, tentatively, Bataa followed suit. He immediately felt extremely uncomfortable, not with the seat itself but with the sitting position. The seat was reclined so that one could, in a relaxed posture, comfortably look up at the projected holograms. He'd been spoken to directly by a navy Commodore in the past and he had stood next to a Lieutenant General once, so, he was having some difficulty with the 'kick back 'n' relax' in the presence of a Field Marshal and an Admiral. His anxiety instantly ramped up as the Admiral steeped her hands and turned her penetrating gaze on him.

"You were originally with the ninth fleet, Admiral Choi-Tan, Basche, is that correct?"

"Yes, Ma'am." Why was his throat suddenly so dry?

"Well, welcome to the second." She gave the slightest of smiles. "I've always taken a personal interest in Guardsman teams who bond and are combat ready in less than seven weeks; these are the most successful and long-lasting. So, what is it, cohabitation or marriage?"

Without the slightest hesitation he answered, "It's a marriage, Ma'am." That's what having instincts do for you: especially when dealing with female-brain emotions that are 13.5% faster and stronger than you are.

She turned to the women. "Thariyan, Heye?"

"Marriage, Ma'am," they answered in unison, 'smiles of delight' in their tones.

The Admiral stood and glancing around signalled that all present were to stand. "Where none exists, I also like setting legal precedents: Rukshana Thariyan, Bataa Basche, and Lara-Tilly Heye your polygamous marriage is duly noted and officially recorded."

When the Admiral sat back down and everyone followed her lead, Bataa got a sense that the ceremony, brief as it was, wasn't anything new to the OpsCen personnel. So, he was officially married, was he? Well it just so happens that he had a platinum wedding ring for each of his wives. What would his dads make of all this he wondered? Funnily enough he didn't have to give any consideration to his mother's views: she would be incandescent with rage - they weren't real women; they couldn't give him children…

"We don't know where the Bulge came from or where they've gone. Nor do we know their strengths or disposition." The Admiral was back to gazing penetratingly at him. "We don't even know *what* they are and I, for one, do not intend to sit around waiting for answers to drop into our laps by happenstance.

The holograms that had been displaying symbols, letters and numbers changed to show a star cluster.

"When we've run into them it's usually around M class planets, but I suspect that's only because *we* have been mainly concerned with the M class. The boffins have identified some prime real estate in this quadrant that they conjecture may have piqued the Bulges interest; G class planets, or moons orbiting super giants that are effectively G class. In the next seventy-two hours we'll be back up to full strength and together with the ninth and fourteenth fleet we are going to visit each and every one."

Was it politic to ask questions of an Admiral of the Fleet? Back up to full strength? Already? After limping away from a walloping, the ninth fleet would usually find somewhere quiet to lick its wounds for a soothing three or four months. Then again, he supposed that as the first commander to achieve any success at all against the Bulge, Admiral Akobundu-Tan would have been given first dibs on resources.

"After each planet is swept and given the all clear we'll need a canary in a coal mine just in case the Bulges make a belated appearance. The leave-behinds will be my most integrated Guardsman teams."

The admiral paused, obviously to give him time to absorb this. He knew that a canary was a bird, a type of flying animal on Earth; he didn't get the reference to coal mine though. More intriguingly, when did Admirals start giving personal orders groups to subordinates that had barely crawled onto the bottom rung of the food chain? He gave a respectful nod signifying that he had comprehended.

"To see if your team is up to the mark, you'll need to evade a simulated Stinger seek and destroy mission for fourteen hours." The Admiral then casually waved a hand to one of the officers over to her left. "Colonel Novalta, the hunter."

How, in God's name, had he managed to completely miss the all in black Gold Stinger sitting amongst them?! The Admiral was so imposing she had commanded all his attention, that's why; he hadn't even given the Field Martial a second fleeting look. Now that he was looking at her, he figured that Colonel Novalta couldn't have been more than a metre and, maybe, a half tall. Not only that, he couldn't help the feeling deep within his bones that, despite having a really childlike appearance, there was something not quite right about her - something utterly chilling lay behind that innocent countenance. Involuntarily, his head started flicking back and forth between the Admiral and the Stinger.

To begin with, he couldn't quite put his finger on it, but there was a definite yet ill-defined commonality between the two women. Then it gradually dawned on him; it was nothing to do with their mutual diminutive seize or anything... physical. There was an aura of amoral lethality emanating from each of them as if they shared a sort of latent malevolent disposition... With the Admiral her, callous fierceness was cannily veiled, firmly under control and highly focussed but still there... He sat bolt upright. Holy fuck, the Admiral was also a Stinger!

With a slight knowing grin at the corner of her mouth Admiral Akobundu-Tan leant forward, and regardless of his sunglasses, he felt her peering into his very soul. He sat virtually paralysed as she held his gaze for several more seconds then she sat back with her smile broadening just a tad. "Scrub simulated seek and destroy mission, we've got our next insertion team."

***

Malachi seemed particularly pleased. "She's always looking for what she calls the 'X' factor. Yours is the first team that she hasn't made jump through that particular hoop. Impressive."

'Jump through which hoop in particular? And why would one want to jump through a hoop anyway?' They had just re-entered the Bay, so he simply nodded despite having no idea what the man was talking about.

"Your target planet, well, actually a moon, has been selected: point 93 G, mainly a carbon dioxide atmosphere, embryonic flora and no fauna of any significance, will be the second the battle group sweeps. If we don't encounter any hostiles beforehand, you'll deploy approximately three days after the fleet jumps: work up until then so let's go check out your BED." Malachi led them past their kit and the Hopper they'd arrived in.

It was probably not in the thousands, but it certainly had to be hundreds of times that Bataa had been in a Bay. In every single instance he had been on route to or from a Hopper that was about to leave or had just returned from somewhere: he'd never actually had the luxury of leisurely wandering around one. *Pantheon* was obviously a battleship and the size of Bay 27 was on par with that of a carrier. Never having thought about it before, it occurred to him that the ceiling was very high: Bay ceilings were always high. You could easily stack maybe six or seven Hoppers one on top of the other. Obviously, some of this space was so the Hoppers could manoeuvre before landing but, even so, that didn't fully explain this surfeit of headroom. Evidently Bays were designed to accommodate something considerably larger than Hoppers and Ground Support Fighters.

He spotted a couple of BEDs about three hundred metres ahead. About twice the height and three times the width of a Hopper they looked like squat bungalows, which was pretty much what they were. Back in the day, there was jubilation at discovering accessible Earth-like planets: playing on Mars and the Jovian and Saturnian moons was all well and good but here were proper Earth-like planets. It wasn't too long into their first crack at settling on one that the Saps had their preconceived ideas on colonisation blown clean out of the water. Assumptions that any rocky planet with 'life', an oxygen/nitrogen atmosphere and ample water would do, didn't survive the first serious attempt.

Even with all the *essential* ingredients in abundance on an Earth-like planet the limiting factor was, and will always remain, the Saps' narrow operating range. Take gravity; +/- 12% one G tolerance: prolonged exposure to any more or any less had profound epigenetic effects affecting a whole range of factors including foetal development. Plenty of oxygen in the atmosphere, fantastic, but at 7% carbon dioxide concentration the Sap starts suffocating and keels over. And that's really mild compared to its evil twin, carbon monoxide, which incapacitates the Sap at 1% concentration. UV in the sunlight, atmospheric pressure, pH norms, mean temperatures, etc, etc: vary them even slightly form Earth's and after only limited exposure, at best, the Sap slides into bad humour and needs hospitalisation.

An obvious solution to the acclimatisation problem was bioadaptations: after all the Saps had the wherewithal - quick, easy, and cheap - to tailor at the genetic level. Then some killjoys drew attention to the inescapable biological fact that if the Saps went down that particular road it would take only eleven generations until hybridisation. During the ensuing 'so what?' debate, other killjoys drew attention to another inescapable fact: throughout recorded history the Saps had demonstrated a remarkable penchant for killing other Saps who parted their hair the wrong way.

The emerging consensus was that it ought to be considered bad form for the sons of Earth to go running around the galaxy dispatching each other with the same gay abandonment they had done when they only had the Earth to play with. But, as always, there was a small minority who said that with all that real-estate out there, they were ready to do whatever it took to put down roots and woe betides anyone who tried to stop them. The majority said playing around with the human genome, except in the strictest of medical circumstances, was immoral, illegal, and just plain wrong so woe betides anyone who did. These *differences of opinions* simmered for decades, with only the odd scuffle here and there.

Because the non-bioadapted Saps were so fragile and Earth-attuned, Earth subtropical became the standard for the human race as it started to expand beyond its solar system. All environmental operating parameters on all spaceships; lighting, gravity, humidity, temperature etc. were always regulated to Earth subtropical. Even on planets, no matter the external environment, the Sap rested their weary heads - physical and mental housekeeping being undertaken during sleep - in a multi-compartments BED. Each self-sealing compartment had independent life support that was set to Earth subtropical. The energy demands to maintain this state of affairs, especially sustaining one G inside a planet's gravity well, were such that most BEDs ran on geothermal power.

On the thirty-seven so far settled Earth-like planets and moons, most colonists' 'villages' were situated near readily accessible geothermal sources as opposed to sources of water like on Earth. The thirty-seven settled new worlds had been more than enough to keep the Saps fully occupied. Then Generation One of the bioadapts had the effrontery to think that they might like to start breeding. The 'hybridisation problem' emerged from under the carpet with a vengeance and the powers that be decided that there would be no Generation Two. So, with the first round of interstellar gloveless fisticuffs in the offing, with ironic elegance and impeccable timing, the Bulges showed up.

Malachi brought the group to a halt outside the nearest BED. "Here's yours: four compartments and because Armour doesn't need anywhere near the same level of creature comforts, scandalously spacious." All five of them paused to regard the Benign Environment Dwelling (BED) with a critical eye and then Malachi gestured them towards the entrance. "Why don't you pop in and check out your new home?"

Bataa stood momentarily hesitating as a quiet, inner voice cautioned about female-brain emotions while Lara-Tilly and Rukshana practically charged towards the entrance. As he unhurriedly followed, the same inner voice hinted that he ought not to say much or offer a strong opinion on anything to do with the interior. The first compartment of all BEDs was airlock and decontamination. Not that the Saps were particularly susceptible to extra-terrestrial biological infections: one area where they weren't so fragile was their immune system. The decontamination was usually for more prosaic matters. For example, the soil on Trolus was relatively acidic and even when wearing an external environment suit, the dust still somehow managed to penetrate and accumulate on the human body in locations where boils and rashes were exceedingly uncomfortable.

With no actual decontamination drills to perform he followed the two women, *his wives*, past the bulkhead into the next compartment which was obviously a well-stocked storage area... This wasn't scandalous at all, it was obscene. This single compartment was as about half as big again as the family home he'd shared with his mom, dads and two siblings. Tight lipped, he slowly proceeded through the compartment and it became apparent that this spacc was not just for storage it was also a repair shop and fuel dump. Taking his time, he entered the next compartment nearly a minute behind Lara-Tilly and Rukshana. Equally excessively spacious this compartment was the communal area and appeared to contain every conceivable domestic mod con...

"Is your marriage exclusive?" Malachi asked very quietly having silently sidled up from behind.

'*Exclusive*?'

"On *Pantheon* we're a commune. When off mission we informally shuffle partners, you know, variety."

Even with their acute hearing he was pretty sure Rukshana and Lara-Tilly were out of earshot, and, seemingly satisfied now moving purposefully into the fourth compartment.

Sensing that Malachi was becoming edgy waiting for an answer he started to feel somewhat aggrieved that his inner voice would choose that precise moment to desert him. He was fairly certain that, ultimately, his Armor would acquiesce to any decision he made. He was equally sure that they'd have very firm, if unvoiced, views on matters such as this.

"We're exclusive." Always best to go with the safest option. Malachi's question had distracted him in the midst of his unconscious mind attempting to handover something to his conscious awareness. What…? It was the domestic gadgets and gizmos; no screens or LED displays - everything was mechanically operated. As he turned to enquire, Malachi answered.

"You'll be going in real old school, complete electronic silence."

"Then how will we be able to…?"

"The 'flares' will be nuclear-tipped, plasma drive, mechanical rockets. We're fairly sure they can't hit a target travelling at even Mach 2 if it has no electronic circuitry. Once clear of the atmosphere the warhead detonates initiating a precisely cascading neutrino shower. Detectors, within a ten light hour radius, secreted elsewhere in the system see the shower and raise the alarm with a repeating superlight broadcast.

Bataa didn't need Malachi to explain repeating until the Bulges found and destroyed the transmitters. That took care of the raising the alarm bit: if the Bulges show up it would be a maximum of, say, twenty hours until the fleet knew about it. "How will we know the Bulges have arrived if we haven't got eyes in the sky and are electronic silent?"

"You must've noticed that the Bulges always make their appearance mobhanded; always discharging heaps of ultraviolet radiation when they enter orbit. And if they decide to come down, as you've no doubt experienced, their antigravity fields tend towards overkill. There'll be chemical UV detectors and some very sensitive mechanical atomic balances - should they make an appearance you'll be the first to know while being virtually invisible to them."

Beaming, Rukshana and Lara-Tilly re-entered the compartment and came up to them. "Cosy," Lara-Tilly informed them.

"What's your best guess of the likely mission length, Malachi?" Rukshana asked.

"The Admiral hasn't shared those thoughts with me but, providing we hook your BED into a suitable geothermal source, you have supplies to last twenty-two to twenty-six months. Your waiting mission is to explore and assess the moon as a suitable forward base." Malachi glanced at him before continuing with a wry smile, "By the way, you can move your stuff in and bunk down here until we jump."

That's a point! He turned to Lara-Tilly opening his mouth to ask the question but she took his hand and said faux maternally, "No, we don't need to but we'll sit with you and hold your hands in the Jump Suite if you like."

With Malachi turned and heading for the exit, Rukshana came up beside him and patted him on the arse. "Good boy, we're too hardwired into you to be 'shared' with anyone else."

Exactly how much information can be conveyed by a pat on the arse? It would seem quite a lot: he was being disabused of any 'sharing' leanings he might have and also forewarned that were such doings ever to occur in the future there would be 'consequences'.

***

"Biocontainment shielding up! Stand by for one G in five... four... three... two... one! Lock down over. Jump medical teams stand down."

Despite him looking crossly at her, Lara-Tilly helpfully held up a sick bag to his face and kept it there. If he could have summoned the energy, he would have attempted to snatch the bag out of her hand. But, as he'd been reminded after the last Jump, even under the most favourable of conditions, her reflexes were a tad faster than his and seconds after a super-light jump weren't favourable conditions at all for the human nervous system.

Easing himself out of the couch he headed for the Suite's exit and resisted the impulse to set off for Bay 27 at the double; that was the old him and so Air Cav. Instead he strolled into the corridor and sauntered along exuding haughtiness as if he were, singularly, the most important person in this sector of space. At the same time, he was very relaxed and contented that the glares and latent hostility emanating from the Suite's other exiting occupants was directed at him and not at his armour following dutifully behind. As they approached the Bay entrance, he simply instructed the door to open and, despite knowing it ought to obey his directions, he was still surprised that it did.

Their destination moon had been swept and given the all clear; the BED and Bulge warning systems were already installed planetside. Now all they had to do was get suited and ride a Hopper down to their new home. Without a word being spoken, they stripped and didn't waste any time in suiting up. As he followed them on board the Hopper, he speculated that he was now completely familiar with the operation of his Guardsman's combat suit but the Air Cav in him was having difficulty taking the laser seriously. Disdainfully holding it at arm's length he considered the thing an anaemic peashooter. With hardly any power to speak of it didn't really merit the name 'laser'. He doubted it could do more that prick an enfeebled enemy…

"Little boys with big guns react and respond differently to little boys with little guns. Remember that a Guardsman's primary role is Recon." The Admiral's voice reverberated around the Bay. *"Good luck on your mission, Tripwire II."*

It took a supreme act of will to stop himself from looking wildly around once he realised they'd been under scrutiny. Rukshana and Lara-Tilly weren't so together; they both reacted like they'd nearly jumped out of their synthetic skins. He'd outcooled a couple of robots… Or had he? His inner voice cautioned that this could be just for effect, 'his girls' stroking his ego.

He waited until they were all strapped in. "Destination Rho Two Nine, VII, landing zone three, launch when cleared."

"Destination Rho Two Nine, VII, landing zone three. Clearance received. Launching."

As the Hopper lifted, Lara-Tilly perkily turned to him, as perkily as one could manage when enclosed in a combat suit, and said, "I think we should call him Steven."

"What?"

"Rho Two Nine, VII - the seventh moon. Seven/Steven, geddit?"

"What effect does drinking alcohol have on you?"

"None and I hope you're not suggesting that my judgment has been, in anyway, impaired."

"In that case we'll have to mark the Seven/Steven proposition down to a software glitch."

"OK then, you magic up something more apt."

"Actually, Rho Two Nine VII, works for me." Was he becoming inured to the contrived banality whenever they became anxious?

"Actually, at only point 93 G, I was thinking of calling him Stumpy," Rukshana added wistfully.

He affected a dramatic deliberating pose, and through the faceplate a staring-off into space expression. "Word 'round the fleet is that combat engineers, because of their unrestricted access to fabrication apparatus, are always totally off their faces on the psychedelics they manufacture." After a suitably long pause, he continued as if thinking aloud, "It's not inconceivable that some of these concoctions could have a marked effect on the quantum computing brain."

"So, you're not enamoured with 'Stumpy'. OK, how about Lowlow…? Mind you, that does sound a touch feminine."

"Lowlow verses Rho Two Nine VII? Why is that even a question, I wonder?" he muttered to no one in particular. What he needed to get done was to bring an element of seriousness to the deployment because as soon as they touched down, it would be standard operating procedure to initiate a combat sweep of the immediate environs of the BED. He wasn't certain that when it came to pisstaking facileness, pure intuition could beat raw computational power; he was one hundred percent sure that in matters of sentiment it would win hands down. "If you insist on a departure from Rho Two Nine VII, I really don't see how, in these circumstances, you can beat 'Honeymoon'.

"Bataa," Rukshana began solemnly, "I know that you'll have difficulty accepting what I am about to say but here it is anyway: I am a conscious, sentient existence and I love you."

The last, and only, time someone had told him that they loved him (in a romantic sense) was the night before he lifted off-planet for basic infantry training. Mengesha, his sanctioned sweetheart - he'd been optioned by the local 'seniors' and both their parents as one of her potential husbands - had tearfully looked up into his eyes and said it, and he believed her. The problem this presented was, in order to get a modicum of privacy they'd left her parent's BED. If this 'moment' had occurred on Earth they could have simply undressed each other and done something about it. Although one could dispense with a respirator for up to an hour or so, at dusk the temperature rapidly started heading towards its minus fifteen degrees night time mean and getting naked on the ground would have resulted in mild acidic burns - this was Trolus after all. They simply ended up hugging each other tightly…

"Let's get down, finish the combat sweep, wait for the fleet to jump and I'll *show* just how much I love you." Lara-Tilly interjected rather assertively.

Jealousy? If they were programmed to be like real women, even women from a polygamous world, he supposed, there would still to be a trace of that. Plus, if you invited sentience to the party it would turn up with its sidekick ego, wouldn't it? And you didn't need intuition or being the sharpest knife in the draw to know to 'never take sides'. "So, is that a 'yes' on Honeymoon?"

"Of course," Lara-Tilly answered neutrally.

"Sure," Rukshana agreed in a letting-it-go-for-the-time-being tone."

As the Hopper entered the atmosphere his intuition gave the nod to 'a truce' rather than 'end of hostilities'.

Chapter 5

Although Honeymoon's gravity was only 0.93 G it had a slightly larger diameter than Earth. This, he guessed, meant that its core was smaller or consisted mainly of lighter metals than Earth's. The undulating landscape surrounding the BED was a uniform carpet of creamy-yellow moss-like flora that was usually no more than a metre tall. This wishy-washy plant life was down to Rho Two being the K3 baby in a trinary of stars and if it wasn't for the vast amount of carbon dioxide in the atmosphere the moon would have been much colder. Wherever the ground was exposed the earth was bright orange. He knew that had it been red in colour that would have indicated high concentrations of ferrites. Which metal's oxidised form was orange?

The combat sweep had taken them well past the three pairs of siloed plasma drive rockets. The batteries had been positioned in a triangle at about a hundred and fifty metres from the BED. Close enough for him to suit-up and manually launch them in a timely fashion in the event of an emergency - of course his wives wouldn't need to suit-up at all. The first set of UV detectors was placed a few paces away from the entrance with many more positioned about the immediate environs. To avoid being disturbed by the site's activities the atomic balances were sited hundreds of metres beyond the silos and would need to be inspected three times in every twenty-nine hours that Honeymoon took to orbit Rho Two Nine.

The sweep lasted the best part of five hours and was systematic because they'd walked it as opposed to bouncing about or using the suits' antigravity. They now had in-depth knowledge of the terrain plus alternate sites and fall-back positions in all directions around their new residence. Bataa suspected that as soon as they entered the BED things would kick off between the two women: nothing really serious or mission threatening just a clearing of the air and establishing a woman-to-woman pecking order. With the fleet long gone and with it all sources of advice, was this was something for him to manage or would the smart move be to just leave them to it? By the time they were a couple of metres from the airlock he hit on the idea of feigning being, with some justification, too tired for whatever jump on his bones form their 'contest' would take.

He was just starting to feel pleased with himself when… it was more a case of feeling rather than hearing that all too familiar percussive boom. "Scatter!" He'd already kicked in the suit's antigravity and was airborne with the laser's targeting systems coming online by the time the second syllable had left his lips. "Rukshana, rocket to the north, Lara-Tilly, east!"

Without checking how they'd reacted to his commands he had covered half the distance to the rocket at the southwest corner of the triangle. Because electronic silence was in force, the suits' radios were locked off, so they had been using good old fashion sound amplification to talk. With fire raining in, and the distance between them increasing, verbal communication was now a nonstarter, he simply hoped that they'd have enough sense not to make directly for the rockets.

Bulge fire, with its booming blasts and ground eruptions, had always put him in mind of ice volcanos. Now he was flying through supersonic chipping and orange dirt so dense that visibility was less than a metre. He'd been in enough firefights to assess that this was seriously heavy shit they were putting down. As he landed momentarily to make his final short jump to where he reckoned the rocket would be, a blast knocked him backwards with such force the suit's gyros failed to compensate and he went tumbling through the air.

For a fleeting moment he thought he had been hit but then it occurred to him that *if* he had been hit, he wouldn't be thinking. He didn't know exactly how a plasma drive rocket worked but it seemed reasonable to assume that a pair of them brewing-up would detonate with the force of a small nuke. The suit's HUD confirmed this speculation by reporting that the external temperature had spiked at over a thousand degrees. Then the suit's automatics took over to ensure that between them, the gyros and antigravity, they arrested his uncontrolled gyrations and placed him gently feet-first on the ground.

A by-product of the missiles brew-up was a momentary scrubbing from the air of the Bulge induced dust storm. He had always thought that carbon dioxide was a non-flammable gas and, according to the briefing summaries, Honeymoon's atmosphere was ninety-seven-point nine percent carbon dioxide. Yet a quick scan revealed that everything in a radius of a hundred metres or so was scorched or still blazing. He was hazy on the exact chemical processes involved but whatever was triggering the oxidation must be stripping oxygen atoms from carbon dioxide molecules.

Also of note was the scorched or still blazing area completely devoid of Bulge fire, just beyond that boundary the attack continued in full, business as usual, swing with a high density of dirt geysers erupting ten, twenty, thirty metres in the air. Interesting… The BED took a direct hit and, as always with Bulge weaponry, it detonated from the inside out - the entire sleeping compartment ruptured in a discharge of heat, flying fragments and a flash.

He'd seen enough and been stationary for long enough; two extended antigravity assisted jumps through the orange fog, unremitting fire and projectile gravel ricocheting off his suit to roughly where Rukshana ought to be. Just as he was about to touch down from his second hop, he got another dose of the rockets brewing-up treatment. He went with the flow and allowed the suit's automatics to deal with it. As soon as he stopped whirling, he made a couple of indirect jumps, heading for Lara-Tilly's rocket battery. This time he was buffeted by a blast that was an order of magnitude less severe. The suit-reported temperature spike suggested its cause was the aftereffects of a rocket launch.

Assuming one of the fire sticks managed to make it out-atmosphere and do its thing, *all* they had to do now was evade the Bulges and survive for the next twenty hours, or so. Where were they? They would have worked out, by a process of logical deduction, that he'd made for the third rocket battery. What they should now do was bug out and regroup - that's what they 'should' do. What they both 'would' do was go off mission and start searching the south west, their aim being to find and protect him. The reasoning that you can't protect anything inside a killing zone wouldn't have impinged on their quantum computing minds. He turned, took a couple of building momentum steps and jumped all the way back to where he'd started - fucking machines!

He saw Lara-Tilly as soon as he cleared the still very much in evidence fog boundary; it was as if there was a force field separating the two zones. Then he spotted Rukshana a couple of hundred metres over to the left. 'Don't stand still, frequent changes of direction' had been drilled into them during the work ups, yet here they were executing a standard search pattern. Miraculously the Bulge fire hadn't returned to the burnt area; if it had, charred bits of both of them would be liberally sprinkled all over the place.

He landed next to Lara-Tilly. "Regroup Shallow Gorge." Then he was gone. He got to Rukshana in three jumps. "Regroup Shallow Gorge." Bouncing away, he set off on an oblique course to the direction of their destination and almost crashed into one of the iridescent mauve coloured alien mounds that was halfway through squeezing out a Bulge. Instinctively opening up with the laser, he set about both the mound and the semi-hatched alien. He didn't know why he bothered; he might as well have been shining a torch on them. This was an escape and evade situation: kicking the suit up to its maximum running speed he set off in one direction then made a sharp turn and brought its antigravity into play.

Running away like this was really pissing him off. On the Omega Zero Three operation they had, for the first time, taken it to the Bulges and chalked up a decent body count. They now had the wherewithal to kill the fuckers! Yet here he was hightailing it, because of this useless poxy laser, as they'd done on so many other occasions. He had been so focussed on the gelatinous enemy mass he'd ignored info the HUD was feeding him. Standard info like the location of friendly forces: the HUD was appraising him of the fact that Rukshana and Lara-Tilly were a couple of metres behind and either side of him - fucking machines!

No point in staying angry, their reflexes were fast enough to keep station as he made random directional changes while putting distance between them and the BED. They arrived at the reference point by taking about eight bounces in about fifty seconds - there didn't appear to be any following fire. Shallow Gorge was a slight depression three and a half kilometres northwest of the BED where the moss-like vegetation seemed to be slightly deeper and denser than the norm. They hadn't been tracked and/or pursued there. Switching their suits to full conceal-and-recce mode they hunkered down to observe the BED and its environs.

Two shrinking mounds were oozing Bulges as fast as they could, and the Bulges were whizzing about the place with their bizarre super-fast, spasmodic movement. He'd been in enough firefights to know, instinctively, that there was something odd about this particular Bulge excursion. For a start he'd never seen two of their iridescent, mauve blobs in such close proximity to one another on the ground; both were less than two hundred metres from the BED.

With them racing all over the place it was difficult to tell exact numbers but he'd say there were between fifteen and twenty-five Bulges, and despite their random motion they all remained within a radius of about a kilometre centred on the BED. He'd never seen, or heard of, that many of the enemy in such a confined space. They were ripping the place apart with the most intense fire he'd ever seen: they seemed intent on annihilating every square centimetre of soil. How were they avoiding friendly fire? The area that had been incinerated by the brew-ups was still fire free, why? Despite this unrelenting barrage they'd only managed one direct hit on the BED.

How could they miss the largest most conspicuous thing for kilometres? Bulges obviously had sense organs, but they definitely didn't have eyes. It always took them some time to zero-in. That's why you didn't want to be hanging around for too long because they always zeroed-in in the end. They bracket a target then rained in fire and, from what he was witnessing, they did this even when the target was slap bang in front of them. This was his first opportunity to, in a state of relative calm, scrutinise Bulge weaponry and tactics; usually he'd be desperately trying to stay alive. For a start there was the fire itself: it was like an explosion without there being any projectiles, rays, or explosives - just a flash and things flew explosively apart.

Zooming in to dispassionately study the relentless bombardment around the BED, it suddenly dawned on him that Bulge fire must target a three-dimensional area, somewhat like a shotgun. The disruptions in the air probably weren't visible. Even if they were, bits of atmosphere flying apart, why would you even noticed. It was the eruptions on the ground that you paid attention to. However, from his vantage point it was now clear that a lot of the detonations were happening below ground and at varying depths. So, to take out something as large and as conspicuous as a BED you needed to obliterate a three-dimensional area thirty times its size? Seriously imprecise and woefully profligate.

Or, perhaps, the BED wasn't that conspicuous or obvious to a Bulge. This BED was supposed to be all-mechanical, but the Bulges were obviously homing in on and targeting something. In reality, it was highly likely that despite everyone's best endeavours there was some instrument or component in the BED that had an electric current flowing. If that thing had been in the sleeping compartment and been damaged or destroyed it might explain the lack of further strikes. This would mean the prevailing doctrine that Bulges preferred going after things with a strong electronic signature needed updating - they could *only* go after something with an electronic signature. This made a weird sort of reciprocal sense because many of the Saps' instruments couldn't detect Bulges, in their varying forms, unless they were in motion…

He felt someone fiddling with the back of his suit then something was connected to it. "What are you doing?"

"Air and water dump. We don't need as much as you," Lara-Tilly stated matter-of-factly.

"The BED is going to be toast soon enough and with it all our supplies," Rukshana added.

His thought-controlled, fly-by-light combat suit was solar/ambient temperature powered and could extract oxygen from the carbon dioxide atmosphere almost indefinitely. Its water recycling was so efficient that even his perspiration and the moisture from his breath were being collected. They both knew this, so this was some sort of symbolic gesture which he really didn't have time for right now. Also, in conceal mode the suit blended perfectly into its surrounding; not quite invisible but difficult to distinguish even when standing next to it. Yet here they were wasting energy on trivialities instead of observing the enemy. "Stop fucking about you two and the next time I tell you to do something, just do it!"

Before either could respond Rukshana's prediction came to fruition as the central compartment of the BED blew out with such sudden violence it shredded the airlock partition to bits as well. A smouldering partial framework was all that remained to even suggest that there was ever an intact BED present. *'OK, you got it. What you gonna do now?'*

The Bulges, in their usual frenetic fashion, started charging into and fusing with the mounds. Note: they did it only one at a time; each Bulge took approximately thirty seconds to be absorbed which was about three times as fast as it took them to bud. As they added Bulges, both mounds started stretching upwards becoming thinner, wiggling and transforming into columns as they did. Without magnification they looked like a couple of mauve coloured strands of spaghetti swaying in the wind. Note: the attack, start to finish, lasted about seven minutes but if all they wanted was the BED that ought to have been accomplished in seconds. Note: the Bulges still avoided the scorched area.

As the columns continued their wiggling elongation skywards it became clear that not all the Bulges intended to fuse with them. Seven of the sixty-metre long, two-metre high, iridescent mauve, worm-like creatures were heading off in random directions. They'd stopped shooting up the place which, he guessed, meant they were sweeping the area for something. Another thing occurred to him: he'd been on the night side of the Omega Zero Three firefight so had only seen silhouettes or night-vison images of the wiggling enemy columns. Now with the naked eye it was abundantly clear - the elongating columns looked *exactly* like Bulges except they were now a couple of kilometres long.

When the columns shifted colour from iridescent mauve to neon blue Bataa knew what to expect next. Both slowly started rising erratically, like immense fluttering neon blue ribbons. The area for several hundred metres surrounding them was being affected by their anti-gravity field. They rose blanketed in a haze of dust, chard earth, creamy-yellow moss, and orange dirt. Note: they might have some miraculous way of avoiding friendly fire, but they were definitely being affected by each other's antigravity. If he were forced to, he'd say that they were actively working at avoiding being drawn together. His suspicion was confirmed when both columns put on an impressive surge of acceleration, ditching their escorting fog of debris, and slammed together entwining. To polish off their party piece they then vanished into thin air.

"Did you see that? It might explain how they managed to ambush us." With no immediate response from either of them his first thought was, *'Still sulking'* but then he sensed that both women were puzzled - no intuition. "We checked all the atomic balances during the sweep - nothing."

"So?" Rukshana's tone managed to convey a convincing shrug.

"Our ships can't make a super-light jump near a mass like a respectable sized moon or planet, but they just jumped while still deep inside Honeymoon's gravity well…"

"I'm not certain that what we just witnessed can technically be classified as a jump effect because ships radiate huge amounts of energy when they enter the super-light - there was no radiation on any EM frequency," Lara-Tilly interrupted.

He reminded himself that it wasn't only their hearing that was souped-up. "Who knows how their ships work? If they can super-light jump out, they can super-light jump in."

"That doesn't explain how they found us so quickly. Nor does it explain this: the entire system was swept by the fleet before our deployment so how did they even know we were here? What was their equivalent of canary in a coalmine? And, a minor point really, what the hell do they want?" Rukshana posed directly *at* him, like he ought to have all the answers.

"A more pressing matter is putting some distance between us and those seven Bulges. Although it doesn't look like it, that manic chaotic hurtling about is what they do when they're searching an area."

"Why don't we stay here in maximum concealment mode?" Lara-Tilly suggested.

"Too many unknowns. Maximum amplified line of sight is about eighteen kilometres so let's head for the high ground to the northeast and observe from there. If the Bulges are actively looking for us it also increases the area they have to search by several orders of magnitude."

"OK, sounds like a plan, but speak for yourself lover boy, we can easily stare eighteen kilometres without tapping into the suit's binoculars," Lara-Tilly concurred.

"I never had you down as a show-off... We'll move singularly, full stealth mode, short low-level multi bounce stages, Rukshana first, then me. Any change in Bulge activities, freeze and assess. Questions?"

"Ten 'o' clock, about one and half klicks, fist shape knoll. Seen?" Rukshana asked.

"Seen," he and Lara-Tilly answered in unison.

"I'll make for the outcrop ten metres to the left of it. Seen?"
Again, they both confirmed then Rukshana was gone, she wasn't even registering on the HUD.

A huge underground detonation about seventy metres in front of them signified that the Bulges had been alerted to something. The subsequent series of eleven detonations, all in divergent directions to Rukshana's destination suggested that, even by Bulge standards, they were way off the mark. The seven Bulges had upped the ante in their dashes though: surging at speed that now must be in the hundreds of kilometres per hour they'd then come to a dead stop or abruptly changing direction. Before you knew it, off they went again; no rhyme or reason to anything they did.

"Let's sit tight and see what develops."

"Why? It's a bog standard, laid down, procedure to move, and keep moving, once they opened fire," she countered.

The acid test of truly understanding any rule is the innate ability to recognise when it is not only acceptable but also desirable to break it - intuition! "Rukshana is obeying orders and I don't think they'll be able to detect us if we're immobile." *We can't spot each other unless there's movement - a reasonable inference.*

"OK."

No come back, no arguing. Good, because he needed to get his brain in gear. The number one downtime diversion aboard ship was speculation as to whether a Bulge was as machine or an organism. From his very first engagement with the enemy he'd been firmly in the 'machine' camp. After all, a sixty-metre long, two-metre high, two metre wide worm that could manage a respectable hundred plus k.p.h. and execute a thirty-five G change of direction/stop - had to be a machine. Now impassively watching them and, inexplicably, he couldn't help feeling that what he was observing were 'creatures'.

Several sudden detonations vaguely near where Rukshana ought to have been signalled that she'd probably moved. Not only that but he could sense that Lara-Tilly was starting to fidget. This drew attention to the simple fact that a quantum computing brain must perceive time differently to an organic one. In their world time didn't fly by when fully occupied or drag when bored - a minute was always a minute. In the Air Cav a 'Freeze and assess', was understood to imply a sit tight for at least ten minutes; with them it was open to a 'how long is a piece of string' interpretations. "Break to the northwest and take a circular path to the target outcrop. Ten to fifteen minutes between bounces."

"But I shouldn't leave…"

"Just go!"

A single detonation seventy metres to southwest indicated that Lara-Tilly had moved from beside him. But as the Bulges tended to spray it around, a single shot meant… He cranked up the suit's audio amplification to the max. "If you don't do what I say they'll find Rukshana and kill her. Move!"

Seven wildly dispersed eruptions of earth being blown skyward signalled that she was complying. Now with Lara-Tilly drawing/deflecting the Bulges from Rukshana and whatever timescales she was operating to he eagerly settled down to capture what the Bulges did next... What the fuck! His eye were telling him he'd just witnessed two of the Bulges ramping-up the speed even further and inexplicably charging head-on at each other. Yet, instead of the expected massive collision and subsequent pileup they somehow miraculously managed to, if he wasn't going to doubt his senses, meld in a sort of passing through each other way. Now, where there had been two, there was only one Bulge with the same cross-sectional proportions but twice as long.

Common sense said there could have been no conservation of momentum in that crash; a fundamental physical law had just been broken. If they could break one, why stop there? The instant accelerations and directional changes could be explained *if* they were reading a different page in the book of classical and quantum mechanics. This was what Recon was all about; he was about to double check that the suit's eye-tracking recorders had captured the collision that wasn't a collision when the Doublebulge started waggling then leapt about fifty metres into the air. The fact that it was accompanied by a cloak of the surrounding detritus on its upward journey would seem to indicate that Bulge antigravity was at work.

Next the rubble smog was falling to the ground and Doublebulge was nowhere to be seen. The suit's acoustic sensors registered the report of a double-clap sonic boom. From rest to faster than the speed of sound in an instant - impressive! He was far too enthralled to be bothered to calculate the speed of sound in this atmosphere. Obligingly the suit was again forthcoming; Doublebulge, maintaining roughly the same height above ground, travelled at two thousand, seven hundred and eighteen kilometres per hour for fifteen point seven kilometres then - without slowing - executed a one hundred and forty-two degree turn, accelerated to three thousand, two hundred and twenty-three k.p.h and had now disappeared from sensors behind a range of hills thirty kilometres to the east.

He was absolutely sure that what he was witnessing was brand new intel, but what did *he* make of it? Single Bulge - infantry; Doublebulge (or dwarf column) - aircraft; dozens of

Bulges, a column - spacecraft. Yes, it was pure speculation, but it made sense to him, if anything about the Bulges could be considered to make sense. He reassessed and then dismissed the dwarf column speculation because Doublebulge was still iridescent mauve while columns were always neon blue. The remaining five Bulges were charging about the place as usual and, clearly, Doublebulge could sweep an enormous area. So, the smart thing to do was just hunker down and wait it out.

That would be the smart thing but what would his Armor do…? They would continue to act on, and act out, the last instruction they received - make for the high ground to the northeast. The not inconsequential fact that a flying Bulge negated the basic reason for wanting to 'head for the hills' in the first place wouldn't have made the slightest impact on their witless quantum computing brains. What was he going to do? The bones of a crazy plan popped into his head. But first: when the opposition's game changer strolls onto the field, it was time to change the game.

He made it to where he'd estimated Lara-Tilly ought to be with two antigravity assisted bounces that were accompanied by the customary way-off-target enemy fire. Switching off the suit's concealment he placed a fist on top of his head, the 'to me' signal. Looking around he hoped she had enough nous to realise that they couldn't *see* her if…Oh, fucking machine! She'd unconcealed and was about thirty metres from his previous position, evidently having circled back to take up her 'protection' post. Tapping his fist on his head, he kicked in conceal mode for a couple of seconds, switched it off and tapped his fist again.

She disappeared and the Bulge fire confirmed that she was in motion. The suit informed him that Doublebulge was making an east to west dash at three thousand, three hundred and twelve k.p.h on a trajectory a kilometre or so south of his position. Pulling off an abrupt ninety degree turn to the north it screamed past, followed by its associated sonic boom, almost overhead - the ground erupting detonations continued unabated way-over-there. It was accepted doctrine that Bulges couldn't fire when in mound configuration. Interesting! What if they also couldn't fire in Doublebulge state?

With sound amplification he'd heard Lara-Tilly's approach before she appeared on his right. Biting down anger, he stated matter-of-factly, "You can't protect me if you're not where I expect you to be." Satisfied with his impassive tone he continued, "Freelancing will simply hasten my death... That goes for you too, Rukshana."

Rukshana appeared on his left and equally dispassionately suggested, "Why don't you make it easy on all of us by not sending us off on wild goose chases when *all* we want to do is stay close in order to guard you, Guardsman?"

Insight: stop thinking, and acting, like the leader of a three-man covert mission and start thinking of Rukshana and Lara-Tilly as simple extensions of himself like, say, an extra pair of hands. No, better still, think of them as extensions of the armoured combat suit that kept him safe in hostile environments... Hmm, so, sentient *armour* that one can have sex with. He guessed that, despite the blatantly overt hints, there were just some lessons that can't be taught; he simply had to get there in his own way in his own time… Now to the execution of his half-baked scheme.

"Here's the plan: *together* the three of us make for the scorched area round the BED and hide in plain sight."

"Apology accepted but I won't be able to keep up with you, I was hit coming over and it's taken out the antigravity," Rukshana informed them pragmatically."

He wouldn't think twice about abandoning a piece of his suit, so the notion of them as sophisticated equipment was only so much bollocks, wasn't it? "Injuries?"

"Nothing to speak of but the near-hit was on the left side; everything else is functioning but AG is down."

"Do you both know what a three-legged race is?"

"Sure," Lara-Tilly answered puzzled.

"Yes, and I know where you're going with this so it's a big no to that!" Rukshana stated emphatically.

"Oh, you've got to be kidding!" Lara-Tilly 'got it' then added, "Don't be so fucking stupid."

"You seemed to be under the erroneous assumption that we were having a discussion. So, to repeat for the final time; when I tell you to do something, just do it!"

"I know we're in the middle of 'combat situation' *boss* but it is not an act of insubordination to voice concern about a strategy that is tactically unsound - all three of us would be at risk of being taken out by a single hit." Rukshana's tone stressed how reasonable she was being.

"We'll make it together or not…"

"Bataa, please stop this Air Cav self-sacrifice shit, we're not programmed to survive without you," Lara-Tilly cut him off.

"What?!"

"Armour cannot outlive its Guardsman," she replied as if that should have been screamingly obvious.

"Are you attempting to remove my combat helmet so you can take a massive great shit in it?!"

"No, Loverman," Rukshana continued to stress just how reasonable she was being. "If you die or are wounded beyond recovery we simply shut down."

Fuck it! Rancid Roger wins out again! Fall in love with them and you'll never make sacrificial lambs of them - check.

But if you love somebody you just might take a bullet for them so… If you die, they die - checkmate. Bastards!

"OK, individually, we'll make for the overcooked bit of terrain swiftly but tactically."

"Nooooo," Rukshana said soothingly while trying not to laugh. "You'll go as a recently married couple on your honeymoon and I'll play catch-up."

About half a kilometre to the east, Doublebulge blasted past heading southwest at a rate of knots. "OK, full concealment on, let's move!"

He reached the bare patch of burnt ground about forty metres from where the BED used to be in five jumps. The Bulge fire, though still wildly inaccurate, was the heaviest since they'd taken out the BED. Did this mean they were becoming desperate? Restless? Frustrated? As he unconcealed he wasn't in the least surprised to find Lara-Tilly unconcealing beside him - there were some things his Armour were exceedingly good at. Rukshana arrived about twenty seconds later taking up position on his left. Sitting and leaning back to back, they formed a tringle that gave three hundred and sixty degrees of visual cover.

His best estimate was that the five remaining Bulges had stepped it up and were now giving it the max to an area about six square kilometres centred on the BED. He'd seen Ground Support Fighters zone and concentrate their fire, the effect was somewhat similar to this: except most of what the Bulge were unloading detonated underground so the blasts were upwards as opposed to outwards and he could certainly feel the nonstop tremors through his arse. As he suspected there was still no activity of any kind in the scorched areas surrounding what was left of the BED. His wasn't to reason why, he just had to accept it as so and take advantage of the phenomenon.

With no breeze to speak of a fine mist of yellow orange fog was gradually filling the atmosphere that Doublebulge would, on a fairly regular basis, tear through leaving a distinct shockwave trail. By any human standards, the Bulges' stratagem was chaotic, slapdash, and eye-wateringly profligate. Yet there was a pondering inevitability about it all - they would find and kill what they were on the hunt for in the end. He was pretty sure he'd read a quote along the lines of 'Quantity having a quality all its own' or some such thing: this could have been said with the Bulges in mind. What about them conserving ammo because even a battleship had a finite amount of ordnance? That would depend on how much ammo, or energy bars or whatever the Hell they used, each Bulge carried in the first place. Plus, what percentage of that total each weird explosion that was not really an explosion expended...

For no particular reason Rukshana suddenly swayed. This momentarily unsettled their little tripod, but she was back erect, as if nothing had happened, before he could react. He gave her the opportunity to explain but she was studiously trying to pass this off as inconsequential... Because they didn't have brainwaves as such, their suits weren't thought controlled, they reacted to micro movements. So, if her suit swayed she started the movement.... Hmm, she'd been assiduously keeping her left side hidden from him. Was Lara-Tilly party to the deception? Probably.

Springing to his feet, he yanked her up spinning after him (so easy to accomplish when wearing a combat suit). There was a palm size hole, like someone had taken a bite out of her suit, below her left armpit and copious amounts of her cream coloured blood was flowing out of it... Fucking machine!

"There is nothing you can do about it, so I didn't bother telling you. Please, let's sit back down and stop drawing attention to ourselves?" Pre-empting him Rukshana plopped herself back down.

He followed her back down. "But…"

"I told you it wasn't worth mentioning, didn't I? We no longer have the facilities to repair me or the suit. The loss of blood is limiting mobility on my left side, that's all!"

"Shouldn't we staunch…?"

"I've already shut down and internally cauterised that area, stop fretting," she murmured soothingly.

Lying: he'd never had reason to ponder whether it was an art or a science. Now he knew the answer and Lara-Tilly's silence on the matter also spoke volumes. So, what was he going to do about it? What scheme could he concoct to compel her to comply with his wishes? Why was he so distressed by her being wounded? If it had been Spam, someone he'd been very close to, would he have been anywhere this anxious? No, he was first and foremost a combat soldier and thus mission focussed. Dead, dying and badly injured comrades were just part of the rich tapestry of the infantryman existence. Yet here he was deeply worried about someone who wasn't really a person and who didn't feel pain in the usual meaning of the word. This was getting a touch uxorious…

"Bataa, snap out of it!" Lara-Tilly suddenly chimed. "Apart from being superlative between the sheets, we were built for this and so are a lot tougher than your average girl." Then despite having her back to him she added, "So Mr. Man, will you please chill."

He almost smiled. They were right about one thing; he needed to stop stewing over something outside his control and focus on the mission. Assuming they had the ammo, and kept up the same rate of devastation, he figured that the Bulges would take another hour or so to total the area around the BED. It would be about twilight by then; would that have any effect on them or what they did? Would they continue to eschew the scorched areas for all that time?

"Here's the escape and evade plan: they look like they may gradually return their attention on this neighbourhood, so if anything hits *any* burnt area we immediately bugout heading north and keep going for as long as we're able to - it's what the fleet would expect. Lara-Tilly with me, Rukshana make as best time as you can manage."

"Sounds like a plan," Rukshana confirmed.

"OK, you call when it's 'time to move'," Lara-Tilly agreed.

Screaming in from the southeast, Doublebulge came to a dead stop about half a kilometre east of their position. Again, Bataa found himself querying the reportage of his eyes: surely it was impossible for an object traveling at a velocity to come to a complete stop without a period of deceleration. What if the Bulges weren't reading from a different page but from a completely different book? A haze of silt sprung up to surround the now wiggling Doublebulge as it sank to the ground. It blasted apart into two Bulges which instantly receded from each other at a rate of knots. This was exactly the same as their merging but in reverse. Was it possible that all the energy from the crash had somehow been stored for all this time and was released in their separation? *Definitely from a different book.*

Why ditch Doublebulge? Aerial search, nothing found, so back on the ground to…? *If* they couldn't fire in Doublebulge mode, this could be to add fire support to their efforts on the ground… The intensity of Bulge fire all around the area went up a couple of notches as the seven of them went tearing about the terrain in the vicinity of the BED. When already saturating a zone with fire, why ramp it up? Although nothing was landing especially close, the fire was now so intense that it was like they were sitting through a mini earthquake. He couldn't help feeling that the bulges were doing this because they were under some unknown time press…

The faceplate blacked out as he felt himself suddenly being upended skyward in Honeymoon's 0.93 G gravity. Hmm… not a direct Bulge hit because he was still here thinking. This was a bit like the rocket brew-ups *but* not the same. Though unlikely, what if Rukshana's combat suits had malfunctioned and exploded? Naw, he had been right next to her, he wouldn't survive either. After cartwheeling in the air for a couple of seconds the suit's automatics landed him on his feet. His faceplate began to clear just in time for him to witness at about kilometre and a half distance an enormous, ten storeys high at its apex, fireball exactly where a Bulge had been heading. It was like the creature had charged headlong into the explosion. A few second later he was lightly buffeted by the diminishing force of the blast's expanding shockwave.

Scanning a three sixty arc revealed the aftereffects of another five similar explosions - not even a bit of one of the huge sixty-metre-long Bulges was to be seen. His eyes came to rest on Lara-Tilly, about a hundred metres away, kneeling over a prone Rukshana. That was deeply distressing in itself; it meant Lara-Tilly had already satisfied herself that he was uninjured and safe to the extent that she'd made her way over and could now devote attention to her… co-wife. He could easily reach them with a single bounce but no, first things first. Under the electronic silence condition of the deployment the radios had been locked off.

The manual five-step drill to reconnect was deliberately protracted to prevent accidental transmission. His fingers, of their own volition, had already completed step three - he really ought to get over to Rukshana.

Step five! "… *Confirm. Over. Tripwire II, sit tight, sit tight! Confirm. Over.*"

"This is Tripwire II. Sit tight, confirmed."

"Roger. Extraction in fifteen or less. Hang on in there, Tripwire II."

Banishing any surfacing thoughts pertaining to the aftereffect of breaches to a combat suit's integrity whilst in the interior of firestorm, he took a slow reluctant pace towards them. Something on the horizon beyond captured his attention, then he looked to the sky. It was still broad daylight, but the heavens were a smorgasbord of dazzling flashes, multi-coloured streaming contrails, and glittering starburst. Intellectually he knew this was the terminally fatal consequence of an enormous low orbit firefight but, with this rear luxury of unhurried gazing, he was taken aback by the feeling that this aerial panorama was the most beautiful thing he'd ever witnessed.

He'd only ever been in a firefight on a planet where the Bulges were bugging out; launching their columns skywards which then combined to form one of their supersized spaceships. Now high above them he could see several dozens of the neon blue enemy ship appearing: this he deemed rather unfair because that was a damn sight more than had departed earlier. Unwinding into what looked like fluttering confetti the ships began to come apart. Had he wished to add to his downheartedness he would have used the suit's magnification to confirm that each of the beautifully shimmering slivers was, in fact, a two-kilometre-long alien column that was heading, with the usual Bulge spasmodic movement, inexorably earthward. There was, however, a modicum of good news in this skyscape because the Bulges didn't appear to be turning up completely unimpeded. Although he couldn't see any Ground Support Fighters, ferocious fire was raining down on the 'confetti'.

He should have felt happy about the fleet's repost but, call it hubris if you must, as far as he knew the only objects/objectives on the planet that could possibly be of interest to the Bulge was, well, him and his Armour. Plus, the last time we'd handed them their arse on a plate they got really surly, threw their toys out of the cot and totalled a whole planet. Hmm... Systematically scanning horizon to horizon confirmed his worst fears. The enemy ships weren't coming down en masse and planet wide as they had in every planetary assault he'd heard about. Instead *all* their ships were assembling in the sky above the BED - this did not auger well.

He landed beside Lara-Tilly in a single AG assisted jump. "We've been ordered to sit tight. Bring your radio back online." Taking a breath, he summoned his, 'Don't even think about arguing with me,' tone. "I know she's dead but we're not leaving her so let's make ready to Casevac; the Hopper won't want to hang about."

"We don't have to, her suit is still functional, I'll slave it to mine."

If he hadn't known better, he would have sworn she sounded submissive. Lara-Tilly stood from her kneeling position and Rukshana's suit followed in getting to its feet then it moved to stand closely behind her, mirroring all her movements.

"Bataa…"

"I don't want to talk about it!" Looking skyward, and all Hell was breaking loose up there, was a convenient distraction. Things were clearly hotting up: of the emerging enemy ships about a third took massive hits as soon as they entered normal spacetime intra-atmosphere. These ships instantly fragmented into thousands of the kilometres-long columns - this was an abrupt flying apart like a mini explosion rather that the systematic unravelling of the ships that had emerged unscathed. Most of the columns turned to a rust colour and started falling like stones but the ones that remained neon blue inexplicably recombined into a new ship.

Why? You'd imagine that being hit would simply be a cruder means of facilitating their separation. But no, any ship that took a direct hit always recombined into a less significant ship after the splintering: then it would try the orderly disentanglement all over again.

There must have been tens of thousands of the columns engaged in their erratic descent overhead. Even so, they were taking so much incoming fire; lasers, hypersonic missiles and, if he wasn't much mistaken, railguns, that not many of them were going to make down unscathed...

"Lara-Tilly! Left side of the BED. Crater. Seen?"

"Seen."

"Freeze Rukshana's suit, back up to it and slave your suit to mine then stand by." He went to stand behind Rukshana's and waited until the HUD signalled that Lara-Tilly's suit was slaved. Reaching under both of Rukshana's armpits he grabbed a firm hold of the backpack on Lara-Tilly's suit. "We're making one jump directly into that crater. Ready...Go!"

Clearing the overhanging piece of the wrecked BED, they landed in the dead centre of the crater. On closer inspection he was now dubious about exactly how much actual protection this battered frame would give. Then again, even unimpeded he and Lara-Tilly wouldn't have made it out of the impact zone. This had to be better than nothing, he hoped: he didn't know how much a column weighed and he didn't want to find out when one came crashing down on them.

"Unslaving." She examined their immediate surroundings then added, "Lie down and we'll add an extra layer of protection for you."

The heavy emphasis on 'for you' defused any desire he had to argue. Lying on his back he realised that he had a reasonably unobstructed view of the sky. The incoming fire was so intense that the upper atmosphere directly above them was beginning to glow crimson, reminiscence of an Earth-like sunset. Higher still the wreckages of human ships were burning up in the aptly named thermosphere. With this much devastation being wrought, it had to be the full complement of the second fleet up there; *and* the total complement of the second fleet was the amalgamation of the third, fifth, ninth and fourteenth fleets. All this to save his little ole arse? Naw, he'd looked into the eyes of Admiral of the Fleet Akobundu-Tan, there were wheels within wheels at play here.

Lifeless columns started landing like very loud and impactful rain, invoking thoughts of what thunderous drumming would sound like. Instantly both Lara-Tilly and Rukshana's suit knelt then arched over him like sprinters in their blocks.

"That looks like it could get uncomfortable after a while."

"Discomfort is a meat concept: I can hold any pose almost indefinitely." She left a suitably long pause before adding, "That's for future reference and something for you to look forward to."

He had several strategies for dealing with the almost overwhelming terror of combat; one of them was diverting his thoughts to matters beyond his immediate, and usually dire, situation. He tried to follow where she was leading but couldn't get any traction: sexual thoughts were still too emotionally charged. He usually went for something far more prosaic; something along the lines of his solo, tension-relieving, long, getaway walks from the cheek by jowl conditions of his home back on Trolus…

"Tripwire II this is Green Monocle. Over."

"Tripwire II. Send. Over."

"Take cover! Eleven, repeat, eleven enemy columns landed in your locale. Excoriating the area in ten…" Lara-Tilly and

Rukshana's suit dropped to lie across him. *"Five, four, three, two..."*

That was all he heard as his senses were assailed and overpowered by a roaring pandemonium, severe buffeting and, if his faceplate hadn't blacked out, no doubt blinding lights. The nearest thing they had to tornados on Trolus were three or four metres high dust devils, but his Earth-centric education ensured he knew what a tornado was. And for the next thirty-three point seven seconds it seemed like he was caught inside one made up entirely of fire and plasma. The suit sensors went crazy and he could feel Lara-Tilly and Rukshana's suit straining to keep him pinned to the ground.

"Tripwire II, Hopper inbound. Approaching from the south. Fly-by retrieval. Over."

"Fly-by, from the south. Roger... OK, get off me." As soon as she complied, with Rukshana's suit mirroring, he sprang to his feet to face south. After that maelstrom he really didn't expect to see any enemy but right there, less than a hundred metres away, was a kilometres high column transforming into a mound. "Green Monocle, this is Tripwire II. Contact! There is...!"

Beams from three independent aerial directions, scorching the atmosphere along their paths, doused the transforming column in a merciless torrent of laser fire. Gradually turning a dull red colour, it slowly toppled over; fortunately, its downfall direction was away from the BED.

"Tripwire II, Green Monocle here. You were saying?"

Why were Atmosphere-jockeys always so damned cocky? Slinging the less than useless laser across his back and taking up a wide stance to expedite the fly-by lift, he checked that Lara-Tilly and Rukshana's suit had also 'adopted the position'; they had. Turning again to the south, he expected to see the Hopper approaching at a height of fifty metres doing a steady two hundred k.p.h. which was the norm for a lift. What he actually saw was the Hopper with about a dozen Ground Support Fighters in close attendance. He'd survived over fifteen combat drops; he knew the drill. Fighters with, 'If it ain't one of ours, kill it!' chutzpah always stayed up top. Only Hoppers came downstairs and got dirty. No, he wasn't buying this: he, and his armour, didn't warrant such overindulgences, they simply weren't that important…

A Stinger's combat suit had souped-up firepower, a Guardsman's souped-up protection; what else did it have? Calling up the suit's diagnostics he had a quick scan: massive memory, in fact it would be more accurate to say his suit had a stupendous amount of memory, what's what. This wasn't news, he'd known about the overabundance of storage capacity, but this detail hadn't seemed significant at the time of learning. The diagnostics also showed that there had been a complete info dump between all three suits as soon as the electronic silence was lifted. And, of course, a suit configured for Recon recorded *everything* across the *full* electromagnetic spectrum.

Now the approaching formation made perfect sense, was in keeping with his assessment of 'her that was in charge' and, perhaps perversely, was much more palatable - the meat was expendable, but information was precious. The tractor beam yanked him off the ground and he was immediately followed by Lara-Tilly and Rukshana's suit as they started their swift skywards assent. Although he was feeling pretty phlegmatic about his suit (and the info it contained) being more crucial than his life, an idea had begun to germinate that he could already tell was going to be one of those ideas that would refuse to lie down… If the desired outcome had been an electronically clean BED, the result would have been an electronically clean BED… *Tripwire, my arse… Bait!*

When about ten metres from the Hopper the rear access opened, and they were pulled in. He had just enough time to strap in while noting that four other suited individuals were already on board before the Hopper's automatics informed them, *"Stand by for high G manoeuvres. In three... two... one!"*

Despite having experienced it many times the fierceness of the aerobatics still took him by surprise. Then again, the G's he was experiencing was nothing compared to what the Bulges underwent. The Hopper must have been in a jinking near vertical climb, the screeching wail of the aerodynamic drag was slacking off as the acceleration piled on, presumably because they were already about to exit the moon's thinning atmosphere. An abrupt eerie silence signalled that they'd made orbit, but this was only a pretext to pile on the G's. Squinting through tear-filled eyes the HUD showed 18G's and climbing. An appropriate animal from Earth came to mind, an elephant. It felt like his chest was where one had decided to lounge for its midday sojourn. Hardly able to breathe he kept his eye tightly closed and ground his teeth. Then there was a sudden shattering half minute or so of even more painful deceleration.

Next, without any warning, the pain was gone. His senses must have been really scrambled because as he opened his eyes and took a deeply satisfying breath he heard, *"This is Flight Command, there'll be Biocontainment ten seconds before the jump. Emergency jump in thirty seconds,"* but couldn't for the life of him figure out the significance.

Even when he heard, *"Lock down! Lock down! Emergency jump in twenty seconds,"* he was still confused. Emergency jump? Did this particular 'jump' refer to a superlight jump? Because superlight jumps could only be made in Jump Suites and people got seriously injured if...

"Lock down! Lock down! Emergency jump in 10 seconds."

It wasn't until the artificial gravity abruptly cut and the all-embracing biocontainment-field seized him, pinning him immobile that he fully realised that the Hopper was already inside a ship that was about to jump. Then there was the momentarily blurring of everything, the nausea, the dizziness, and the mind-splitting juddering during the actual jump itself. He hadn't known that it was even possible to travel through the superlight outside of a Jump Suite. What biocontainment? Outside of a Suite and it was worse, much worse - the symptoms were about ten times as bad. Nastiest of all was the 'slap': the harsh return to normal spacetime when everything flashed back into sharp focus like being plunged headfirst into brutishly cold water.

"Biocontainment shielding up! Stand by for one G in five... four... three... two... one! Lock down over. Jump medical teams to Sector six, deck twelve; Sector fourteen, deck five; Sector eighteen, deck nine and Sector twenty-two, deck three."

The Air Calvary never puked! They left that kind of insipid behaviour to the matlows and ordinary grunts. However, as soon as he took off his helmet, Lara-Tilly had the sick bag at the ready and he promptly emptied his stomach contents into it. Any embarrassment at his gastric discharge was instantly mitigated when he noted, also with helmet off, Malachi being similarly attended to by one of the suited figures. That this individual had responded as timely as Lara-Tilly meant that they hadn't been affected by the superlight jump so they couldn't be a 'person' either.

Despite being strapped firmly to his seat, he still managed to sit bolt upright in after-the-fact shock: for the sequence of events he'd just experienced to have happened in the order they had meant that the Hopper must have still been under maximum deceleration when it flew straight into the hanger.

Braking into a cold sweat he slumped back in his seat - automatics were precise but surely not that precise.

"Flight Command, have we RVed with el supremo?" Malachi asked, still sounding groggy.

"*Roger. Flotilla on the move sub-light, have matched velocities and in formation.*"

"Thanks Flight Command, out to you. Hopper, destination *Pantheon*, launch when cleared."

Figuring that he had a number of pressing but conflicting matters to address he settled on leaving the most troubling one until last. As if reading his mind, Lara-Tilly turned her attention from ministering to his needs to manipulating apparatus on Rukshana's suit. Leaving one still fussing over Malachi, the other two suited figures nimbly came across to join her in her endeavours. Meat was never this sprightly straight after a superlight jump, plus Armour didn't vomit so there had been no rush to remove their helmets. What were they doing to Rukshana? He simply did not want to deal with that now, so he focussed on the Lieutenant.

"It seems to me, after much Bulge induced terror, that we were left out as an offering."

Still looking the worse for wear, Malachi gave him a weak smile then seemed to pull himself together. "Most of this is way above my paygrade but have you ever heard of dark matter or dark energy?"

That sounded to him like yet more clandestine outfits. He shook his head.

"Back in the day, pre-superlight, scientist could only account for about five percent of the observable universe. The missing ninety-five percent they postulated consisted of dark matter, matter but not as we know it - about thirty percent. The remainder was dark energy; a repulsive anti-gravity that they thought was accelerating the expansion of the universe."

Bataa did his damnedest to affect a 'You're full of shit', look. No one ever got hung out to dry in the Air Cav.

"*Destination* Pantheon. *Clearance received. Launching.*"

Ignoring this, Malachi pressed on. "That was until the discovery of the zeta neutrinos, which are more commonly known as the bright neutrinos... You have heard of a bright neutrino, haven't you?"

That question was a bit like being accused of being a retard. It was basic high school physics - the super abundant bright neutrino: a lepton with the characteristics of a boson that was its own anti-particle and also mediated both the force of gravitation and the force of the cosmological constant - the particle that made superlight flight possible. He was feeling enough grievance over the death of Rukshana and at being used as a lure to last him several lifetimes, so he decided to let this one slide. He nodded.

"Well, once the bright neutrinos were discovered they accounted for most of the missing mass of the universe. Then everyone got all excited about building superlight drives and pretty much forgot about the anomaly. Yes, bright neutrinos made up 'most' of the missing mass but not 'all' of it. Roughly seven percent was still unaccounted for, but nobody cared because interstellar travel was now not just a possibility but a probability well within mankind's grasp.

"The old school theory postulated that dark matter only interacted with ordinary matter via gravity. And let's not forget that ordinary matter - you, me, this ship, the stars out there - only makes up about five percent if we exclude the bright neutrinos. New school posit that the two forms of matter interact via gravity *and* bright neutrinos." Malachi paused as if to check that he understood; satisfied, he continued dramatically, "This is where, we think, the Bulges come..."

"So, they think Bulges are made of dark matter? The bits of them that I've come across seems like ordinary baryonic matter to me." He couldn't resist bursting this all-knowing little bubble.

Malachi didn't seem in the least perturbed. "It's a yes and a no to your question. The current view is that, yes, the Bulges exist in and are from the dark matter space/realm - at bit like them being from a parallel universe but not."

This was just so much bullshit. "How can they be like being from a parallel universe but not be from a parallel universe?"

Raising a questioning eyebrow at his 'tone' Malachi answered, "If they were from a different universe, they'd have different physicals laws. From the same universe it's the same physics as ours *but* the chunks we don't yet understand. Apart from the not inconsiderable inconvenience of dealing with the Bulges, some people are really excited about that. This 'realm' could provide solutions to some of the thorniest unanswered questions in cosmology such as of why there's more matter than anti-matter in the universe."

He'd never have pegged Malachi as a nerd. "Right. So how is that gonna help us kill more Bulges?"

Without changing posture or expression Malachi fixed him with a stare and simply metamorphosed into 'the officer'. "Feeling sorry for yourself? Then consider this: over three hundred thousand men and women died in getting your arse off that shit piece of rock, Guardsman."

Bataa didn't respond but everything about his demeanour shouted, 'Yes Sir! Understood, Sir!'

Malachi relaxed, a little, then continued, "The thinking is that what we perceive as the Bulges are in fact trans-matter holograms... Or, perhaps, a better similitude would be trans-matter force fields, analogous to controlling iron filings through a sheet of paper with a magnet. The 'magnets', of course, being gravity and bright neutrinos."

While he struggled in choosing his next words more cautiously Malachi continued with his explanation, "You know we think that the Bulges can only use prime numbers?" Bataa nodded in conformation. "Well, twenty-six teams were put down - more, or less, than they would respond to simultaneously. Each Tripwire team 'bled' a unique electromagnetic signal. They bit on three but yours got the strongest reaction which developed into, as you saw, a full-scale assault. By the way, they've now destroyed Rho Two Nine, VII but we've managed to gather a rough guesstimate of the 'broadcast frequency of their *magnets*'. The intel your team adds will help to refine our understanding"

"So, you're saying the Bulges always know when we're around and can drop in on us unannounced because they can play in our 'realm' but we can't play in theirs?"

Malachi looked genuinely please. "That, in a nutshell, is precisely what I've been led to believe."

Repentant and humbled he accepted, yet again, that he was simply a small cog. Over three hundred thousand men and women had been sacrificed retrieving the information recorded in their suits. He had no doubt that the data had already been winged across the airways and was currently being sweated over; any apparently insignificant extract could be the key to unlocking the Bulges. He could also see that Malachi didn't have to personally undertake the retrieval mission, in fact, he would have had to overcome command reluctance and put a bulletproof argument for it.

"I think that it takes extra energy for them to initiate a transformation/merge in our realm, so they have no spare energy to shoot."

The Lieutenant actually smiled. "Save it for the Admiral. As the Armourer no doubt intimated, raw data and algorithms can only take you so far; perceptions, insights and mental leaps are what leads to breakthroughs. Your contribution has been significant thus far and you don't have to believe in metaphysics to *know* that you've had an angel watching over you." His smile broadened. "The Admiral and her Staff Officers will debrief you personally. You're a Guardsman, any intuitions you have will be given credence. This, after all, is a unique and historic conflict."

His confusion must have shown because Malachi quickly added, "This hasn't been a battle over territory, religion, ideology or even something as essential to our nature as bioadaptions. This non-human conflict is evidently a war of fundamental physics. It's a conflagration with an unknown enemy about who will have ultimate control of bright neutrinos: we can't manipulate/exploit them without affecting the Bulges and vice versa."

"*Arrival* Pantheon. *Disembark.*"

Malachi then waved his arms casually to the accompanying women who had all by now removed their helmets: Rukshana had been stripped of her suit revealing her left side, from armpit to hips, completely charred. "Bataa and Lara-Tilly this is, Verity, Sasha, Yana."

Three Armour? Where was it written that there only had to be two? As there were nods of introduction all around it occurred to Bataa that, yet again, here was evidence of commonality - the 'women' were obviously different: different height, build, ethnicity, etc. *but* they had some ill-defined characteristic in common apart from being female. What was... had been the commonality between Rukshana and Lara-Tilly?

"Before we disembark, I'd like a private moment..." He couldn't explain it further and just hoped that they understood or would have the good grace to simply do as he requested.

Without speaking they all grabbed their kit and exited the Hopper leaving him with Rukshana's… corpse? Chassis? How could he be feeling such a sense of lost at a dead android? An android he'd only know for a matter of weeks. *It* was never alive to begin with so *it* could not be dead. One *cannot* suffer bereavement at the loss of a fucking machine! Yet tears were running down his cheeks… It wasn't considered good form to keep an Admiral, not just any Admiral but an Admiral of the Fleet no less, waiting. At a loss of what to do he eventually lent across and kissed her lightly on her forehead then stood to leave…

"That was deeply touching but please stop blubbing." Eyes open, she was staring at him, amused.

This was so unexpected he leapt a couple of centimetres into the air. "You're not dead."

"If my memory core is intact and *you* aren't dead, I can always be repaired and rebooted, I am a just contraption after all… Now get over here and kiss me properly."

The End

INTERDICTOR

ISBN 978 0 9506087 8 1

For decades, Earth's Attack Cruisers have taken a pounding from an undefeatable enemy. An enemy so alien and so incomprehensible Earth's armies are close to utter devastation; clueless as to how to challenge the impending annihilation of the human race.

For the first time in the twenty-seven-year war the enemy has placed a base of operation on a planet and Admiral Ezocaagbo Akobundu-Tan is willing to risk the destruction of her fleet in order to get one man on to that planet, Lume, a highly trained special forces operative. He is also a Stinger, a human adapted for a single purpose - to kill...

PILOT

ISBN 978 0 9506087 6 7

The Explorer Corps' spaceship *Arabia* has the distinction of being the ship that has travelled the farthest distance from Earth. Eight days ago Earth lost communication with the *Arabia*. The spacefighter, *Baddest*, is one of a pair of spaceships that, at more than fifty miles long are the largest machines ever built. *Baddest* is normally crewed by the Air Force's Ace Crew II but for this mission the crew is supplemented by the Navy's Special Combat Team Alpha. The Navy and Air Force are bitter space-borne rivals.

Mission: To find the vessel *Arabia* or to establish, beyond reasonable doubt, her fate and that of her crew.

EMPRESS

ISBN 978 0 9506087 4 3

She was the only one who could reunite the Empire and restore to its citizens the security that this brought. Without any doubt she was, singularly, the most important being alive. She and her cousin were the last of an Imperial bloodline.

But her cousin could not easily supplant her. For Hial to sit on the Imperial throne she would need to be victorious in a bitter and bloody war. Such a war was to be avoided if at all possible. Therefore, the primary task for Empress Morturina I, and those who served her, was to ensure her survival - at least until she had borne an heir to the Imperial throne.

But war was inevitable...

All Woman

ISBN 978 0 9506087 2 9

There you are getting on with your life. When up pops THE blast from the past... The dim distant past - not seen, not heard of in eight years - but there he is. He's telling you the story: 'Sorry I dumped you but having trashed all my subsequent relationships, I've finally come to realise that you are the one for me, we should be together.' It just so happens that he was the love of your life and it also happens that things are more than complicated...

What would you do?

INTERFACE

ISBN 978 0 9506087 7 4

It's the 80's. Clare is white, Patrick is black. They are from entirely different worlds, *but* when they met, they fell madly in love - perhaps opposites do attract. Now they plan to get married.
A straightforward proposition, right?

Well, maybe not. Set against them and their wishes are a host of 'interested parties': Clare's sister, Emma. Patrick's best friends, Harry and Nathan, and his ex-girlfriend, Otis. And of course, their parents want to have a say as well.
All the ingredients for a delightfully outrageous exploration of the *Interface* between: black men and white women; black men and black women; the maturity (or immaturity of men); strong personalities domination of weaker personalities.

Will love conquer all?

There are many books written for women about the pregnancy and childbirth phenomenon. There doesn't seem to be much in this plethora of literature for men. It's about time there was!"- Ray A.

Thinking Man's Guide to Pregnancy, Childbirth & Fatherhood (ISBN 978 0 9526287 3 6) provides a male's tongue-in-cheek perspective of said phenomenon - a humorous slant on all things an expectant father needs to know but is too afraid to ask.

Disclaimer
Ray Anthony makes no claims to having any special qualifications for writing such a book, apart from having been there, seen it, and done it!